The Divine Song

THE AFRICA LIST

ABDOURAHMAN A. WABERI

The Divine Song

Translated by David and Nicole Ball

LONDON   NEW YORK   CALCUTTA

The work is published with the support of the
Publication Assistance Programmes of the Institut français

Seagull Books, 2020

Originally published as *La Divine chanson*
© Abdourahman A. Waberi

Published in arrangement with Agence litteraire Astier-Péscher
All rights reserved

First published in English translation by Seagull Books, 2020

English translation © David Ball and Nicole Ball, 2020

ISBN   978 0 8574 2 694 9

British Library Cataloguing-in-Publication Data
A catalogue record for this book is available from the British Library

Typeset by Seagull Books, Calcutta, India
Printed and bound by WordsWorth India, New Delhi, India

For Bérénice

To Ngugi wa Thiong'o and to Jean-Marc Moura

The only people for me are the mad ones, the ones who are mad to live, mad to talk, mad to be saved, desirous of everything at the same time, the ones who never yawn or say a commonplace thing, but burn, burn, burn like fabulous yellow roman candles.

Jack Kerouac

CONTENTS

PROLOGUE, *or The Melody of Creation*   1

CD 1. *An Evening in Paris, End of April 2011*

    In the Beginning Was the Divine Song   9

    Greedily Tasting the Pleasures of Paris   17

    A Man in Pieces   21

    From Mississippi to Montmartre   33

    The Mystery of the Blues   39

    Occupy New York   47

    The Fatherless Son   59

    The Brilliant Student   81

    Nina Little   98

INTERLUDE. *A Night of Ecstasy and Downfall,*
Berlin, Early May 2011   109

CD 2. *Seeing Harlem Again, End of May 2011*

    Sappho's Thighs   123

    A Six-Dollar Piano   131

    Angel Dust   139

    The Pact with the Devil   150

    Coma   156

EPILOGUE, *or the Melody of Compassion*   171

Statement of Intent, Sources   181

Let's take up the sequence of events again.

My name is Paris. I'm not just a ginger cat. I am the old cat of the prodigy Sammy Kamau-Williams. I'm going to tell you his story in case it has not yet managed to reach your chaste ears. Like my master, I am a son of the open road. We traveled together for many long human years, Sammy and I, leaving our footprints on the summer dust, in the silvery winter snow and in the gold of the yellowing autumn leaves. Our life: the most extraordinary passage through our earth. Witnesses have told us that we were alike, like the two faces of the moon. The comparison does not end there. Just like him, I am shaggy-haired, I have a creative imagination, and like him, I am skin and bones.

For a reason unknown to my mind but obvious to my heart, just a few years ago I couldn't talk to other cats or to dogs. And still less to humans. Some of those creatures would change platforms when I passed them in the Harlem subway. Others, more hostile, would raise their paw, bare their teeth, and try to jump on me, calling me a phlegmatic demon. Or worse still, a show-off.

My name is Paris, and that, too, has come with age. In another life, I was called Farid. I was the Persian cat of Mawlana, a great Sufi master who came from Konya. I was the guardian angel of this holy scholar, who had lived in the warm shadow of God wherever his feet took him, from Samarkand to Shiraz, from Persia to the Maghreb, from Jerusalem to Timbuktu and as far as old Abyssinia, where he rests today in a little cemetery protected by a fence of eucalyptus trees several centuries old.

Paris or Farid, whatever the fur or the name they give me, I am both the same and another.

Under the azure cupola of heaven, I dance, with my head of an avatar, to the beat of the cosmic dance. But my heart has not changed one iota. At least if I am to trust my instinct. Even today, I am thought to have spiritual leanings because I prefer the company of books to the company of my fellow creatures. This is extremely exaggerated, for most of the time I either gambol around in the meadows of my brain—trading my feline body for the profile of a hawk to cleave through the air, or the silhouette of a dolphin to cleave through the ocean—or I doze in my corner, praying in silence and keeping my thoughts to myself. I can remain motionless for hours on end, busy meditating. Sometimes I come back to earth to make faces, roll my eyes, or mew from time to time, adapting my behavior to the requirements of the situation.

As an introvert, I observe the little comedy of human beings, grumble just for the sake of it, roll myself into a ball under the couch, or laugh up my sleeve. As an extrovert, I act the cute little cat, playful and harmless, so I can get myself petted.

But there you are, everything has changed since that fateful morning in April 2011. Nothing in this world interests me anymore. Inconsolable, I take refuge in yesterday and its carousel of memories. And yet, harbingers of the event were visible to anyone with eyes to see, but by pure reflex I turned my back on them. I was afraid.

First of all, sweltering heat, unusual for the season, fell over the whole region. The rays of the sun got the better of the asphalt of Manhattan: the taxicabs left long jet-black furrows under their tires as if they'd gone through the outskirts of Hell. And then, for three days and three nights, a burning wind from God knows where dried out our throats and squeezed our lungs. Finally, the vulture went by, as predicted. Many are those who saw it circling over Sixth Avenue under a copper sky. If a drone had been flying in the area, it would have sent us excellent photos. But that time, I must admit, I was much more vigilant.

I knew the impatient vulture would come back one day or another. And I was lucky enough to follow its circular movements. I saw its rotating dance with my own eyes. It froze my blood.

And there it was.

Imposing and arrogant.

Punctual, as if to seal someone's fate.

But that isn't all. Yesterday, Thursday, May 19, 2011, Sammy the Enchanter was admitted to the St. James Infirmary on the corner of 113th Street and Amsterdam Avenue, at the age of sixty-two. The verdict is unequivocal. His condition is worrisome, even alarming, I would say. My former master from Persepolis would say his fate is in the hands of the Pardoner and that's the way it should be. That's why the Farid I once was would have relaxed on his prayer rug with his head turned to Mecca, but the Paris I am today doesn't know under which star to stand. Nor which way to turn.

I certainly won't bury my clown-like head in the sand, or let myself be paralyzed by fear and forget the main thing. For I, Paris, signed a secret pact long ago with Sammy the Enchanter. If it were up to me, I would never open my mouth, but today I must admit I have no choice. I have, so to say, my back to the wall.

I must speak, round up my memories, and bear witness. Relate the poet's biography, his first lines, his first raptures as well as his first terrors. Retrace all the important elements of his biography here below: his precocious vocation, his poverty in this last decade, his success and his persecutions, his martyrdom and posthumous triumph—if, however, the great and adulated fighter were to go to Heaven before the hour was up.

Our pact stipulates this clearly. I must retie the thread of the past to do battle. For the vulture, the winged beast, the faithful companion of Azrael, has just shown us its claws and its torturer's face. In case I come to forget it in my old age—let me recall in passing that nowadays a cat lives an average of fifteen years in New York as well as in Cairo or Sydney—this reciprocal commitment has been set down on paper, in black and white, and slipped into the hollow of our favorite song.

I must *do battle for his soul and mine.*

As I told you, with us everything begins with a song and everything ends with another song. On a signal, people swing into motion, their solar plexus supplying the necessary energy. They turn and turn, crescendo. Make loops and double helixes reminiscent of the structure of DNA. Refrains rise and are transmuted into particles and waves before slipping into the incommensurable immensity of the universe and last the time needed to stretch out into the expanding universe.

On earth, songs are heard in princely dwellings as in huts where laughs burst out like logs in a fireplace. They are, most often, a gift of grace. An invitation to rise into the firmament. Nothing is lost, nothing is created, everything is transformed to feed the universe. And the songs whirl around ceaselessly in circular movements, melting into stellar fires to be reborn firmly docked to rings of stars.

On the earth of men, they tell a thousand stories about the origin and benefits of their lyrics. They say songs are like a necklace of pearls linked by the thread of infinity. They say they die and are reborn to whirl again like atoms or like the dances of whirling dervishes.

When he was very small, Sammy fell into that cosmic sea and its strange, marvelous depths. His family immediately detected his gift for music, but it would take Sammy twenty years before he offered the public his voice, his guts, and his words. The time to perfect his demanding apprenticeship.

In 1970, to escape the claws of education, my master records a three-minute text with an African drum as its only accompaniment.

"The Revolution Will Not Be Televised" is on every radio station. On everyone's lips, too.

Apotheosis.

Sammy Kamau-Williams enters into legend. He became an icon. An idol for the young and the not so young. Rise, fall, and redemption. He is born, grows up, dies, and is born again in music on the steppes of the media. A classic: thousands of singers, rappers, slammers, and DJs claim my enchanter as their inspiration. And he didn't lift a finger to profit from his aura. He had more urgent things to do on this earth.

What a career! you will marvel, wide-eyed. Just like me, Sammy remained both the same and another. However, one trait of his personality did not change. He is just as thirsty for the ideal as the day he was born. Up to that moment when, on his hospital bed, he's about to meet his Maker. The thirst for the absolute is both his sap and the source of his torments.

With us, everything begins with a song and everything ends with another song. Meanwhile, bodies begin to move, as if to the snap of a finger, joyfully whirling to the rhythm of the Ever-Living One.

CD1

An Evening in Paris
End of April 2011

So if you see the Vulture coming,
he's flying circles in your mind,
Remember there is no escaping
for he will follow close behind.
Only promised me a battle,
battle for your soul and mine.

Gil Scott-Heron

In the Beginning Was the Divine Song

Everything began with the Divine Song.

In the beginning, too, were active, clement words, and those words were accompanied by a melody on the ney, a reed flute still heard in the sacred sanctuaries of central Asia.

And that is how the universe was created, Sammy would say, indefatigably, if he could sit up on his butt, lower his long legs to the floor, or take a few steps in his hospital room.

He would tell in great detail how the pink, lilac day rose over the world. How lands emerged from the waters; and how the stars settled at the zenith, driving the darkness far, far away from us mortals. Plants, animals, spirits, and human beings made their entry filing two by two in order of size from elephants to fire-spitting dragons to earthworms.

Mischievous as they are, cats were the last to get on the clay vessel, singing the primordial blues, the Hymn to the Creation.

I am an old bachelor cat, on the threshold of his last life. You'd think my eight first ones went by just like that, in the snap of a finger, without my being aware of anything at all. The dawns, the months, and the years that were bestowed on me fled so rapidly I thought fate was abandoning me in the open field. And yet I am still in this world, more useful than ever in this auxiliary role for which I had been preparing myself for a long time, meditating on the lessons of my first spiritual master, whose name was Mawlana. He had predicted that my last life would be spent in the wake of an unknown man with strange ways. Devastated by the loss of my preceptor, I didn't pay enough attention to the prediction at the time. I had made my decision: to survive my initiator so I could put his precious teachings into practice. You will live each day as if it were your last, he used to advise me. Before adding that I should savor each inspiration and each exhalation as if they were the last to leave my chest, and I should welcome death with serenity. In other words, I should play my score as swiftly as I possibly could.

That is how I lived through the weeks that followed the death of our venerable mentor. No point telling you I had sworn to remain faithful to my guru by bearing witness to the beauty of the world. Life is beautiful despite its vagaries and my nine lives show this clearly. Life is beautiful on condition that you serve it. In other words, helping others, the brothers and sisters you meet along the way. And for me, that other brotherly face is above all Sammy, the mage who burned his life at both ends.

It takes very little for the whole universe to hang in infinity, to use Mawlana's favorite image, like a song whirling on itself. Very little keeps the wheel of the song turning. Almost nothing makes every creature sing a little tune in resonance with the great universal song. And every infant who comes into the world starts its life with a first arpeggio in the form of a cry, incomprehensible to our insensitive adult ears. And for good reason: we have lost our ability to wonder at the rhythm of the first of songs—the song that goes piously from mouth to mouth, from slope to slope, from planets to constellations. The song that inaugurates the first step in life and gives the world back its waters and the motive for its presence.

The matrons passed the word around. They claim the baby lets out his first cry, which is far from true. He undertakes his journey and knows the secret of the first of songs. Only his mother understands him but she is not always able to call our attention to the first notes of this hymn to Creation. She diapers the baby while trying to overcome the pains of childbirth. The first cry, that new language full of hope, is lost in the noise of the clinic and the clicking of surgical instruments.

You will not be surprised to learn that I was not born in a clinic. I was thrown into the world in a rather brutal way and no one yet knows what the ninth song holds in store for me in the folds of its refrain.

However, I am not superstitious and I don't consult horoscopes. I no longer read coffee grounds ever since my Sufi master gave me lessons in awareness a very long time ago: he listened to the rhythm of my breathing, step by step, consciously, in the paths of a fragrant garden in Nishapur in the east of Iran.

I don't have a watch on my wrist or on a fob like Lewis Carroll's mischievous rabbit but I possess an American passport and a vaccination book, both in a sorry state.

I was not always as good as an angel. My neck has known in turn the caresses of silk and the rigors of exile, the gold of the lucky and the edge of the guillotine. My hands have felt the warmth of ink and the cold of the bayonet. Sugarcane and cotton broke my back and tattooed my flanks with a thousand wounds. My eyes have seen loved ones die and whole cities disappear. My epidermis is a parchment on which time writes, engraves, and hardens. As for the rest, let's say I'm a bit more cunning than Dinah, little Alice's cat, still alive in Wonderland.

Since the dawn of time, man sought out the company of cats because of their sharp senses. The Romans scrutinized their slightest movements to predict volcanic eruptions. Their sight gave them a rather pleasant mix of excitement and terror. It is said that the Sumerians read the sound and germination of time in the pupils of felines. The Akkadians invented an anti-seismic prevention system before anyone else. Shamans interpreted the cries coming from cats slipped into an underground tunnel with a sophisticated traction cable. The prize goes to the pharaohs, for they bowed down to our felid magnificence. At the time of Nefertiti, we were the overlords of the world.

Today's cats, as tamed, vaccinated, and castrated as they may be, have not lost their touch. They know how to make themselves useful in various ways, some known to the general public, others quite secret. I would rather have cultivated humility and remained silent about my modest feats but it's too late for that. I am bound by the pact. My story is waiting to be carted to the four corners of the world.

I must *do battle for his soul and mine.*

It is said that the ocean never lets its fish escape, just as the earth does not let its children throw themselves into the ocean. The sea was enjoined never to go beyond its borders so as not to torment men. There are old rules that regulate the laws of nature and the dance of the universe. As for me, I've put my steps into those of Sammy the Enchanter since the blessed day of our encounter on an almost deserted sidewalk, two hundred yards from Times Square. Here in New York, in the middle of Manhattan, as I'm sure you know.

Inseparable—in fair weather or foul, we became inseparable. I often trot along lazily in his wake. But sometimes I cut out fast because a noise scared me, and when that happens Sammy's the one who starts running like mad to catch up with me. One day, after a

memorable chase, he breathlessly confided in me that
I'm his moon. I replied that he's my sun. We burst out
laughing. A frank, roaring laugh under the eyes of
the stunned passersby. Whether he was serious or in a
joking mood I'll never know. On the other hand, I can
guarantee that I never left him, not even for a second,
for the sun is nothing without the moon, and the moon
nothing without the sun.

We whirl around together day and night. With him,
every single day of my life has meaning again. Our
drawers are filled with projects. He thinks that at sixty
he still hasn't had the time to explore a whole panoply
of musical genres. I agree with him. I concede that he's
perfectly right again and I promise myself to help him
give birth to those songs, choruses and melodies, so
hard to express. I understand his hesitation, for yesterday, everything smiled on him: as soon as he was back
from one of his walks and started scribbling on a piece
of paper, words seemed to flow out of him quite naturally. Today, it's harder.

Sammy's long strides are famous in the Village and
beyond, especially in Harlem, where not a day goes by
without someone stopping him in the street to ask how
he is or greet him at great length. Whenever this happens, the admirer puts his hand fervently over his heart
while bowing his head like a Tibetan bonze. My
Sammy, proud as a peacock, returns the greeting with a
little motion of his head when he's in a hurry or he stops

to exchange some ardent words, burning with brotherly love for the aficionado. Even if I keep at a distance in such occasions, I can read his ruby lips and it takes me hardly thirty seconds to guess the content of their conversation. People worry about him. They ask him again and again why he hasn't come out with a record in more than fifteen years and why the record labels and the radios keep ignoring his precious compositions. Sammy responds jokingly, evoking his long musicological research, and refuses to take his personal situation too seriously. There are so many talented young brothers eager to succeed, he once retorted to Suleka, a young singer who swung her long rasta braids from left to right as soon as she passed her favorite composer in the street. Like her, few admirers notice my presence, even though I'm only a few steps behind him.

I know how to make myself invisible to ordinary mortals, and Providence gave me another gift: the ability to read signs and dreams that people trapped in the incessant, exhausting struggle for survival can't see. They rarely leave the cavern of their bodies, but once they have bread and a roof over their heads, human beings throw whatever strength they have left into satisfying splendidly useless needs: to appear richer, stronger, brighter, and more handsome than their next-door neighbor.

It has now been several weeks since I felt the shadow of the two-headed vulture gliding over our heads. It did give me a start at the time, but I didn't worry too much because we were on tour in France. Nothing really serious could happen to us so far from home, I thought absentmindedly.

There we were, performing in peaceful little cities with exotic names. Cities with a historic heritage and famous wines. Our mission was to spread the blessings of the Divine Song everywhere. That's why I can name those cities in order, without making many mistakes, for they're engraved in my cerebral cortex. We took a bus, then a local train, then the bus again in the middle of nowhere, and finally another train. We roamed the French provinces, from jazz festival to jazz festival, from Cognac to Vienne, to Saint-Tropez, Uzès, and Évreux. Finally, we arrived in Paris, greeted by the acid droppings of the pigeons at the Gare Saint-Lazare.

We spent most of our time in Paris, what with culinary pleasures, rehearsals, and visits to cloisters and museums. I must admit I love everything about this city; the elegance and majesty of its sites speak to me most particularly. Quai Voltaire, the Seine, and the Louvre will never fail to charm me. I love sticking my nose into the innermost recesses of the capital, far from the tourist circuits. Wandering through the fragrant gardens of the Great Mosque of Paris, for instance, sipping spiced tea in the backyard of this sanctuary for virtuous men—these are some of the small pleasures that reconcile you with true life.

Greedily Tasting the Pleasures of Paris

We arrived in Paris by train. We had left New York a week earlier. At our arrival, the month of April was expending its last cartridges and the sky over Roissy had the color of beeswax. Right there on the tarmac, filled with emotion, I warmly thanked Providence for having lifted fear from my heart. Gone were my dread of weightlessness and air travel. I had slept like a baby during the crossing. When I woke up, the rain was in my eyes.

And there we were, safe and sound in Paris, the city my friend and master loves so much.

"I called you Paris because like the city, you have a big, palpitating heart," Sammy used to tease me when he was in a good mood.

Sammy and the City of Light have an old story with each other. Sprinkled with great joys and many storms. A story of hot and cold coming together and mingling their tumultuous waters.

So here I am in Paris.

It was a first for me. Something told me this trip wouldn't be easy. The fact that Sammy had talked to me a lot about Paris, its eternal beauty and its impeccable grace, didn't reassure me, though. I tried to imagine a city that was both ancient and modern, turned toward science, beauty, and the sacred without being too austere. If that were the case, it would have had no chance of charming this troubadour who loves vibrant, convivial and rebellious cities. His companion Sappho did not always share his opinion about Paris but she would emphasize that the city is not what it once was.

When the topic of beauty came up, she'd get on her high horse and say with irritation: "Paris is a mummy, an open-air museum." Once, they held the productions of the mind in high esteem, treasured the works of the past, cultivated artistic talents and sought out the company of words. Beauty was tracked down wherever it was hidden, in the poor neighborhoods and in cabarets. Alas, that Paris is no more than an old memory, she would sigh. The fault of millions of tourists swarming in the belly of the capital and transforming its restaurants and legendary brasseries into dispensers of frozen food, hardly fried, but given enticing names. Traditional cuisine or not, Paris is a long-delayed baptism that is finally happening. What's more, it is on the threshold of the last of my nine lives. I totally enjoyed the Eiffel Tower, the Buttes-Chaumont and the Moulin-Rouge. In Père-Lachaise cemetery, I meditated at the grave of Jim Morrison, who left us at the age of twenty-seven like Janis Joplin, Jimi Hendrix, Robert Johnson, Brian Jones, Kurt Cobain, and Amy Winehouse. Those *artistes maudits* understood very young that half a life and a handful of songs were enough to leave their mark on the world and enter into legend.

Die young and you will be adulated—that's what they seem to be whispering to us, with the approval of the enchanter. If they were prematurely struck down, it's because they were able to feel, early on, the vibrations of the great, telluric song. Before they were crucified in the prime of life. They deserved their ultimate, deep sleep. They command respect, Sammy would think, fighting between life and death on his hospital bed at this very moment.

Paris commands respect, too.

It abounds with Gothic buildings, graves hidden under the cobblestones, earthly clamors in the corridors of the Metro and on the Grands Boulevards where, mixed into the crowd, Afghan fakirs are disguised as flower sellers, Tibetan yogis and venerable master drummers who, in the zawiyas of the Maghreb, lead the faithful into trances, into vertigo, into fainting. I know how to recognize these saintly officiants, but that isn't all.

I want to know everything about Paris.

Taste every bit of it.

I made the rounds of the record stores and jazz clubs and then switched gears to dash off to the Louvre on the double. Great was my disappointment. The Mona Lisa seemed quite small to me, not to say tiny.

Her lips so thin they disappeared under the peak of her nose. Why all the fuss about this woman who seemed to have a permanent squint?

Paris has surprises in store for you.

As a baptismal present, I was treated to an octopus carpaccio swimming in olive oil. I swallowed my artistic disappointment to reconcile myself with humanity.

My name is Paris, as I already told you. The man the press sometimes described as the black Bob Dylan gave me this totemic name because Paris was a synonym for a never-ending party, eternal summer, and the fountain of youth. Because of that name, I get plenty of "wows" in the streets and gutters of Manhattan.

All that is already far away. The vulture has gone by.

As punctual as Papa Legba, the Voodoo Master of Crossroads, the character with a thousand faces in Haitian tales who, like St Peter, holds in his bony fingers the keys to the other world.

A Man in Pieces

There is what is known, bathing in the bright light of noon.

There is also the unknown, crouching in the deepest parts, be it inside us or out. And there are several gates between the two worlds. Ever since he was very small, Sammy knew how to push open all the gates, whether they give onto the porch of azure blue heaven or onto the plaza of hell. A fairy had leaned over his cradle. She was beautiful, radiant. Divine and eternal, too.

Her name is Music.

And she was there for him.

From the first day on, watching over his first steps, helping him to open the gates effortlessly.

It was all settled in early childhood, Sammy confirms to the passing visitor or journalist. Still better, he launches into confession in these terms:

"I was born in Chicago but it's the red clay of Savannah, in the state of Tennessee, that's always been my natural element. My grandmother had bought a cheap piano and every day, early in the morning before I left for school, I got into the habit of assaulting it with my fingers. And under her direction, I threw myself totally into music. It was not only a demanding practice but also, above all, a faithful, invisible playmate. I didn't choose music, music chose me. Made me its ever-vigilant servant. I hope that all my life I will remain the eardrum that vibrates to the chimes of its era."

Humble and elegant—which never prevented him from being ambitious and demanding—since he left the mud of Tennessee behind him, he certainly went a long way. On stage, Sammy always gives the best of his talent in the dazzling light of the instant, gathering the band and the audience around him in the same communion. Every concert brings a new sound and most importantly, something unexpected. Something to surprise everybody: an incident, a touch of madness or the tenacious feeling of days speeding by without warning.

The night before last, on the occasion of his last concert in Paris, the virtuoso lost his dentures in public. The incident escaped everybody. The jazz lovers in the club, and strangely enough even those in the first row, in the pit two yards away from the band, had no idea. Me, I didn't miss a bit of the action. And yet I was in the back of the room. Perched on the windowsill with metal curtains. I saw the whole thing. True, the event didn't last more than ten or twelve seconds. The five other members of the band (Ed Hurley on electric guitar, Rob Fulton on bass, Larry McGee on percussion, Jordan Kim at the piano and Tony LaPierre at the drums) attracted the audience's attention to themselves even when they were turning their back to him.

I'm not the kind who gets easily distracted, whether I'm outside, in the first row at Carnegie Hall, on the roof of a skyscraper or in a rat hole.

I swear I saw everything. At the moment, I felt a pinch in my chest but I also had the strength to record every motion, every fraction of a second. I stocked it all in my feline brain. I can describe every single detail of the scene to you; I can speed up the film, slow it down, or freeze it.

As soon as Sammy realized he'd lost his dentures, the whole length of his body stiffened and time stood still. For the space of a second that felt like an eternity on that last day of April 2011. Then time began passing again, indifferent to the fate of the little Earthlings that we are. And every element got back to its place and its role in the great theater of the little nothings we call life.

The rest went as reported in the papers. The columnists proved themselves to be excellent weavers of rumors. Some drew wings on the dentures, others multiplied their variations on the theme of the fall. And yet none of them were actually present in the concert hall. The Web exploded, spreading waves of gossip. Thousands of "Toothless mouth" emails went around from Tokyo to San Francisco. On Twitter, the discussion thread "#OpenMouthedattheNewMorning" got the most tweets.

The turn this incident took, both tragic and comic, reminds me of an old story my mentor used to tell me in my third life, when I was still called Farid and was a real Sufi cat. Our story is still told today in Anatolia, Tajikistan, and elsewhere in Asia Minor.

"An elephant from the depths of India was cooped up into a dark stable. Full of curiosity, people rushed to the stable. As it was hard to see because of the lack of light, they began to touch the animal. Very soon, they began talking. One of them touched the trunk and said:

" 'This animal resembles a huge pipe!'

"Another touched its ears:

" 'You'd think it was a big fan!'

"Another, who was touching its legs, said:

" 'No! What they call an elephant is actually a kind of column!'

"And so each of them started to describe it in his own way.

"It is really a shame they didn't have a candle so they could all agree."

Although it was badly lit, the New Morning was nothing like the stable of my Persian tale. Things happened differently.

Sammy slid a bony hand down his leg to pick up the denture. That right hand hit the rubber sole of his right foot before it picked up the precious accessory. With the other hand, acting natural with his fingers drawn wide, Sammy kept on playing, drawing out a few sunny notes on a bed of percussion as the audience savored the harmony of the sounds with an almost carnal joy.

In Paris, Sammy was all sweetness. He was celebrating the early summer evening in his own way. In turn solo pianist, composer-writer, singer, poet, and consciousness-raiser. A laugher and a joker, too. Sammy was at the top of his form, doing everything with panache.

If his last mistress, Sappho LeDuc, from New Zealand, had been there, huddled in the semi-darkness of the New Morning, watching over her man like a lioness over her cub, she would have seen Sammy's mouth of darkness open and close with ecstasy, as I did. She would have recognized the liver-colored red gums, the swollen lips, chapped with dark streaks as if a blowtorch had gone over them. She probably wouldn't have taken her eyes off her lover who, after the incident, was playing with both hands, his denture stuck between his jaws and his cheeks less hollow.

His head slightly bowed, his half-open eyes were staring at the floor of the New Morning. He seemed to draw colossal forces from the depths of this club in the

Tenth arrondissement of Paris, halfway between the Porte Saint-Denis and the Gare de l'Est train station. Even though he was weaker, Sammy was as handsome as a prince of ancient Egypt. He had a contagious laugh and a luminous smile. His voice: all of black music. At that moment, you could feel he was *free*. He was there, alive. Visible and free. A free man is always intriguing for other human beings. He gives them the chills.

Sammy radiated grace. He was holding off the vulture's Dance of Death. Standing on Paris ground he felt supported, his doubts and anxiety swept away.

"For me, it all began a long time ago, when I was a tiny child growing up on the red earth of Tennessee. The first initiatory tree grows there on that soil and I am the fruit of that tree. How can I make those pathetic little heads understand that? Wherever I go, whatever I do, their malevolence follows me like my own shadow. I hear their conceit, I live with their scorn. I can read their thoughts as if they were up on a screen. If I'm in Paris, it's to play and reconnect with the audience, for God's sake, but those people will never leave me alone. The only thing that makes them happy is sticking my head underwater. I know their taste for shit, *the same old shit*," Sammy rages into the phone without paying any attention to my simpering airs. His features are more drawn than they were this morning and his black eyes are rounder and burn like coals. At the other end of the line, Nina has found the right words to reassure her protégé;

I notice that his face is progressively regaining its sparkle. Forty minutes later, he wished Nina good night in a calm voice. Nina never opens her mouth unless she has something useful or kind to say.

As he put down the phone, he gave me a weary look. And in a clear, almost overbearing voice, as if he wanted to get back at someone or something, he announced: "I'm going out for a little walk." I could feel he wanted to be alone and that's why I let him take the direction of the Porte Saint-Denis. He needs solitude like a bird desires his nest at twilight. His instinct led him to the street where the half-naked girls pace the sidewalk from noon to noon.

Before I met Sammy, I thought there were two particularly monotonous races in the animal kingdom: men and dogs. I no longer think that way. Besides, I tend to avoid all peremptory judgments. I learned humility, compassion, and the sense of paradox from him. In the course of the same morning, I can go from feelings of empathy to being completely selfish. And smile at everybody as children do. But right now, I'm beginning to be beset by worry. He left in a fury, slamming the door. And I couldn't hold him back. Nor accompany him. To console myself, I remembered that Oriental tale I was told back when my name was Farid—or was it when I had fallen madly in love with beautiful and sweet Shirin?

"As Sunbul Effendi, the sheik of a great Order in Istanbul, was seeking a successor, he sent his disciples to pick flowers to decorate the monastery. All returned with large bouquets of beautiful flowers. Only one, a certain Merkez Effendi, returned with a small, very wilted plant. When he was asked why he hadn't brought back something worthy of his master, he answered: 'I found all the flowers engaged in recollection with the Lord; how could I interrupt their constant prayer? I looked around and saw a flower which was done praying. That's the one I brought back.'

"It was Merkez Effendi who became Sunbul Effendi's successor, and one of the cemeteries at the Byzantine wall of Istanbul still bears his name today."

For me, stories tend to be soothing. When I hear or tell a story—which amounts to the same thing in the end—my breathing becomes calm and regular. If words pour out from my mouth in waves it's because my heart is turned upside down from sorrow. I feel devastated, crushed like manioc turning into flour under the pounding of the pestle. Usually, I don't speak to human beings, whether they are black or white, young or old. I don't trust them. Especially here in New York. I'm wary of men, women, and their mutts. Their kids are worse. They give you a bone to chew and put you in chains for the rest of your days.

With my guide, it's another story. A story of respect and love. We understand each other from a distance.

We caress each other with our eyes. No need for words. For biting or scratching. I am his shadow, the guardian of his memories. I'd give anything to make him happy. If I had his wonderful voice, I would sing his songs, for I know them word for word. Almost as well as he does.

Words pour from my mouth in waves when I am extremely moved and can't control my emotions. Emotions are electric impulses and carry off everything in their path. They go through the magnet of the heart. We have the capacity to feel joy or sorrow for others from afar. Through telepathy.

I am in a good position to know this; I have the same feelings as Sammy and it doesn't matter if I'm far away from him. It's always been that way, at least since I set down my bed or more precisely my litterbox in his little apartment.

"Make yourself at home, friend!"

These were his first words, if my memory isn't playing dirty tricks on me. I found a home, an oasis in his shadow. And I also discovered magazines, records, and books there. With angelic patience, I turned them every which way before reading them one after the other. Reading gives me a sensual pleasure. I felt good in their company. Little by little, my body and mind got used to a new discipline, my organism to a new hygiene, and my senses to new surprises.

I never made a great distinction between traveling and reading. I'm as enchanted by the length of a journey or the pages of a book as I am by the landscapes of my life.

On the road, I stick to my little habits and rituals, otherwise chaos takes over inside us. Always between two states of waking—never really awake, never really asleep, I base my rhythm on the rhythm of the asphalt, I melt into nature. With a little luck, I manage to set down my bed in bright, functional spaces like an architect's model for instance, the kind that don't necessarily keep the wisdom of the world inside a calabash but make it easier for us to live. On buses, I look for a spacious little spot on a rear seat; on a train, I always settle down in the last car.

In the wake of my friend and master, I've swallowed up the miles, I've devoured space.

For Sammy Kamau-Williams, the sweetness of that April evening was only a passing respite, a temporary return to life, a quarter moon before the darkness. We were all in the night; we were greatly in need of rest.

The last forty years of Sammy's life were epic and exhausting. A geyser of sap. He gave a lot. He spent his time rounding up his brothers and sisters and bringing their energies together like those trees that mingle their branches in the sky. Writing and composing with others or solo. Putting bands on stage with Dany Gibbs and other world-class artists. Singing, giving free concerts in the ghettos of Washington DC, Los Angeles, or Dallas. Reaching out and working relentlessly with others to give birth to Revolution. Fighting against the enemy of the day, whether it's called Segregation, Dick Nixon, or Ronald Reagan. And above all, never despair, for the old mole of history would end up by showing the tip of its muzzle.

With every fiber of his body, he wanted to raise his people and leave behind a musical body of work while breaking the joints of the diabolical machine of capitalism. With his words, he succeeded in turning himself into a healer, a prophet, and a leader. A hunter of djinns. And that isn't all.

His problematic bohemian lifestyle and irascible temperament can explain his innumerable enemies and the silent hostility that surrounds him. But Sammy only listens to his conscience, more tormented than his mind. When I open people's eyes to reason, they say I'm insane, he confesses in one of his most famous songs. People in the music business excommunicated him. No matter. Sammy keeps on sacrificing his life for the well-being of others.

The revolution cannot wait. Secession is what we need, he raps out, always vehemently, for white America, as sexy as a cactus, is running to its ruin. It is playing with death *mano a mano*, fascinated by its own downfall. Its lost children like Jimi Hendrix, Sam Cooke, or Jim Morrison got the message hidden in the blues like the almond hidden in its shell. And everyone knows what happened to them afterwards. Had they imprudently revealed secrets too heavy to bear? Did they behave appropriately before the angel of death? What had they seen at the final hour? Did they sing a last tune of their own or recite one of Rainer Maria Rilke's poems as they were about to leave this earth? These are the questions that torment my sorcerer.

Until that evening, the bard's life and work were one identical thing: genius and madness. Heads: fires and hell, fall and damnation, unfathomable abysses and demons. Tails: illumination, music and activism, offspring and strokes of genius. He was also grazed by the wings of angels. With Sammy, no half measures, no happy medium. He steers clear of social events, media coverage, and honors. People admire his boldness, his vigorous playing, his vision, and his charisma. They hate him for the same reasons.

From Mississippi to Montmartre

In living memory—or the memory of a live cat—that Parisian concert was a miracle from beginning to end. I replay the film in my mind to recover the feelings that swept through me at the New Morning. A few minutes after the dentures incident, was he confused, assailed by strong emotions, or was it simply a deceptive effect, due to the purple and vermilion gleams of that temple of jazz? The club opened on the evening of April 16, 1981 with the drummer Art Blakey, inventor of hard bop, playing godfather to the Jazz Messengers.

The unbelievers, who think they can detect the flames of hell in my eyes, are going to make up many theories. I'll let them go around in circles in the dry well of their obsessions.

"New York Is Killing Me," "Sisters of the Yam," "Take the A Train," "Winter in America," "Living to Love," "Ain't I a Woman," "I'm New Here"—he played one piece after another, and as flashbulbs crackled and applause sounded, he regained his confidence. He relaxed, jokingly recounting his problems with the justice system. As ever, incredibly seductive. Teaching, transmitting a tradition, carrying the heritage of John Coltrane, Bird, and the great Billie Holiday.

His "I'm New Here," above all, kept all his promises. The new man was there, so different and so similar. With his soles in the dew, he was totally there.

Haughty and timeless.

Standing upright as if in the first morning of the world.

Between two pieces, he tells fragments of stories. Real or imaginary stories. The blues player turns into a storyteller who also likes to tell entertaining anecdotes. Like Papa Legba, he knows how to stand at crossroads. At the crossroads of yesterday and yesteryear.

And his memory goes back to the source. In the backcountry of childhood. Somewhere between Clarksdale, Mississippi and Savannah, Tennessee, where the blues was born. The sound of Creation was born over there, in the Mississippi Delta. In the muck and mire, in the bowels and acrid sweat of African slaves.

Sammy's cavernous voice enchanted his audience, mostly connoisseurs. Jazz buffs who'd been sucking it up from their earliest childhood. Those are the people who made Paris one of the biggest capitals of *the new thing*, the thing you talk about only with initiates and whose name you never pronounce.

If Sammy hadn't been on tour in Paris, he probably wouldn't have chanced to come across *the new thing* or at least suffer its effects. In Amsterdam, Barcelona, or Rome, in any case everywhere his detestable reputation hadn't followed him, he would have taken refuge, as ever, in those dark places that no electricity reveals. He would be reported missing just as he had been all through the past seven years. Hunted down by his demons, wanted by his creditors. Chased by the FBI and the New York State police.

The gazettes were buzzing with rumors about him. Only yesterday, he was said to have left without saying a word to the French organizers. A whim, or a hoax? They thought him lost in his beloved Paris. Or danger had caught up with him. Or he'd gone out ghost hunting again in the clubs of yesteryear, from the Chapelle des Lombards to the Boeuf sur le Toit. With foaming, blasphemous lips, the Cassandras are predicting his relapse. Purportedly, a shadow with more strength than he has lies in wait for him, or the galactic desert of his own demon has swallowed him up.

Nothing like that happened, thank God. No enemy thrust his bayonet into his long silhouette. Sammy was warmly, passionately welcomed. His public didn't hold his tardiness against him. It would seem people hadn't forgotten him. On the contrary, they'd been waiting for him to return. They hoped they'd see him one last time. They loved him as they had the very first day. I had the time to wink at him as he was sitting down at the piano. He made a little gesture intended for me only. I felt relieved.

When I get an idea in my head, it always comes to me as music and melody. I was born in a middle-class household in Brooklyn. If I tell you my family was white and rich it doesn't really matter, for the difference between men, even in the United States of America, doesn't affect my psychological canvas very much. At this stage, let's say I see them as all the same. Blacks, Whites, Hispanics, or Asians. I owe you another confession: I'm a failed composer. I was a fair saxophonist, I've spent a lot of time with composers, works, and interpreters, but I quickly understood that music was not my thing. You have to know how to accept your limits and your own insignificance in certain fields.

As I grew older, I learned to master my emotions and accept what fate held in store for me every passing dawn. I also accepted my own insignificance in musical creation but I can appreciate other people's talent. What's more, coexisting every day with a genius who thirsts for the absolute like Sammy is no sinecure.

Mind you, I'm in no position to complain today. Especially here in the City of Light. Paris has a knack for making us Americans go nuts, especially our artists. And particularly musicians in quest of the unnamed, unnameable Thing.

The Thing is supposed to have started in New York, where it was a regular in the shady milieu of Greenwich Village. It was seen for the last time sipping a beer at the Five Spot Café, the club of the Termini brothers on Third Avenue. Then it vanished without warning. Evaporated. Gone from the screens. Swallowed by the great night.

A few decades later you find it again in Paris. Initiates put step into its traces against their will, sucked up by the Thing. New disappearance. Since then, nothing solid to get your teeth into. Just rumors, pipe dreams. Theories.

The best sleuths took up the investigation again as soon as the disappearance transpired. They know their business, they studied with the greatest artists. With Charlie Parker, Miles Davis, Dizzy, Monk, or Coltrane. No heroes, no guide among them, just inspectors, patient as stone.

And yet nothing rises to the surface. For some unknown reason, the Thing is hiding. In the country of the "Nouveau Roman," the "Nouvelle Vague," and "Nouvelle Cuisine," its appearances were astonishing. Intriguing. The writers Jean-Paul Sartre, Boris Vian, and all their fellow writers in Saint-Germain-des-Prés were watching for the return of the Thing. For a time, it was thought to have slipped away into the catacombs of Lutèce, not far from the Jardin des Plantes. The story goes that a Haitian living in Paris, a connoisseur who claimed he had encountered the Thing for the first time on the balcony of the Hôtel des Orchidées in Pétionville, may have seen it sneak into the cellar of that club located at 666 Boulevard Montmartre, a club from the period between the two world wars. From then on, we lose its trace. Perhaps it's holed up in one of the clubs where Parisians discovered the following facts, in this order:

The American saviors sometimes were of ebony complexion;

They often had a good knowledge of swing;

Some of them had chosen to live in the capital, like Josephine Baker.

The Thing had felt at home in pre-war Montmartre but in the years 1945–50, it suddenly migrated to the Latin Quarter. On the Left Bank, the Thing became *The New Thing*. Everything becomes a sign or a presage for whoever is on the lookout, ready to marvel at something, to interpret, to imagine concordances and connections. The more it's sought after, the more it plays hard to get. And yet, the Thing is in Paris for sure. A charmer. But still as invisible. Meanwhile, musicians play their music, women give birth, old people die in solitude, watchers of signs are on the lookout for the slightest signal. The Earth turns, but the Thing stays in hiding. Right here in Paris.

The world hangs by a thread on nights of the full moon. It is nostalgic for the Thing. It longs for its return. Still better, it awaits it like you wait for a messiah.

The Mystery of the Blues

It is said that children grow up and adults grow old. When I arrived in Paris, I felt both in the skin of a growing teenager and in the skin of an adult going downhill. I mean I had nothing to complain about, life was sweet. In Paris, the sky was clear, almost white from being so blue. May was the prelude to a torrid summer that would make you forget the freezing winter and the sweetness of spring. And not a trace of the vulture, of that I was absolutely sure. Everything was happening as predicted by Papa Legba, the purveyor of destinies, the one who opens the terrestrial doors.

The Rue du Faubourg Saint-Denis is a microcosm unlike any other. It overflows with energy and invention. That long working-class thoroughfare has its icon and patroness: Madame Eglal Farhi. The owner of the New Morning, from the height of her eighty-nine years, was sitting in the first rows, honoring the return of the prodigal son to the international scene by her presence. She emanated the natural gentleness and elegance of an Ottoman princess captured from life by the brush of a Flemish master.

The concert started forty-five minutes late. After a little round of observation, they found each other again. Sammy and his fans. As in the time before the disaster.

He was making his bet. His name was displayed in huge letters at the entrance to the club on the Rue des Petites-Écuries. For a few days still. An eternity. Thumbing his nose at the spiteful high priests who bet on his downfall. God can be kind to His creatures, as Sammy's grandmother who had survived the great Mississippi floods of 1927 would say with a sigh.

No slipup. Not the slightest threat in view. It was said that nothing and nobody would derail the course of events in Paris. And Sammy was grinning from ear to ear. Pretty proud to have proven the Cassandras wrong. Looking them up and down. Proud, yes, but not vain.

Above all, he was free, joyfully free and in communion with the audience. He was charming, irritating, and intriguing in the same breath as if the words coming out of his mouth were uttered by someone else, were coming from an unknown source buried in his guts. Between two pieces, with his grating voice weathered by a life of excess, he takes his time, makes the pleasure last. Keeps the best for the end. To definitively delight his audience by offering on a silver platter the different levels of interpretation hidden in the Divine Song:

"Each of you understands the Song at a different level, parallel to the depth of your understanding. The great masters of the original blues, the ones I affectionately call *bluesologists*, have counted four levels of discernment. The first is the apparent meaning, and that's the one the majority of people are content with today.

The chroniclers and radio hosts haven't even reached this first level." And the audience laughed in the half-light of the New Morning, the time it took Sammy to clear his throat and go on. "Then comes the inner level attained by people who have opened wide their souls throughout their lives." A pause, the composer's eyes now stare at a point in the horizon as if his gaze were going to fall beyond the invisible line that begins at the last row, where the people not lucky enough to get a seat are standing. "The third level is inside of the inside. The fourth is so deep you can't even put it into words or music. So it is condemned to remain indescribable."

Once he's seated behind his piano, his little nod is the signal for the music to take up its reins again under the applause of the audience.

In New York, the reporters, record producers and radio programmers finally got tired of the singer's eclipses. As early as 1990, Sammy had a terrible relationship with Athena, his second producer who wanted to squeeze him like a lemon. Because he revolted, they said he was lost to showbiz, not cut out for the role of a performing monkey that was served up to him on a golden platter. With juicy contracts made behind his back with bar owners and amusement parks located at the other end of the country, sometimes in Florida, sometimes in California or the Bahamas. Obstinately, he rejected the proposals of the production company, holding the helm like a shipwrecked man holding on to his lifebuoy.

The Athena people hate to be resisted. They took their revenge. To say they're at the origin of the bad press my master and ally received would not be unfair or excessive.

Sammy is portrayed as an unstable person; irascible, unreliable. A rumor exists to be spread around. It is fed by lies, misunderstandings, and gossip.

The rumor goes that Sammy shoots up his whole entourage with heroin and his family suffers a great deal because of it, especially his daughter Dahlia. It was said that he was caught in a luxury hotel injecting his cat Paris. Spitefulness is always spying on celebrities' private lives and knows no limits. Men's minds are such that they wish their fellow men the worst as soon as they are prey to fear, jealousy or covetousness. What can one do? To hide is not possible and to deny is certainly not the most effective method in my situation. What would the word of an old cat be worth against a battalion of handsomely paid lawyers?

My inner eye has never fooled me. Sammy is much gentler and loving than the Brooklyn lady who drowned my brothers and sisters. As for me, I was never tempted by alcohol and drugs. I am accustomed to keep a cool head. Especially in times of madness.

They didn't stop there. They claim his harangues, his humor, and his outrageous political statements are out of date, out of fashion. Worse still, his star is out, dead like the hidden side of the moon.

What's trendy now are danceable tunes, easy to remember, easy to forget. Young people love rap; they want easy money, venal loves, the charms of advertising and self-forgetfulness. On the dance floors, those young people, in love with themselves, feel their hearts go boom-boom-boom and swell to bursting.

But Sammy is an alchemist in quest of the Magnum Opus, the task of a lifetime. Paper is his alembic, ink his primordial fire. He turns away from the boredom of ordinary days that weave the web of miserable destinies. Those poor wretches cut off from any future will perish as they lived: as spectators. Without faith or connection.

For months now he hasn't left his ground-floor apartment. He's waiting for inspiration. He's hoping the angels will bring him a chorus or a bit of melody. It was easier before. Slavery, segregation, revolt, and submission: nothing escaped the chopping block of his conscience. Nixon, the atomic bomb and its ravages and the election of a real cowboy—stupid, cynical, and brutal— at the head of the first country in the world.

Sammy padded the bay window with a thick, purple-colored curtain to make night fall in his long, narrow apartment. Constantly bathed in half-light, it became a place filled with shadow and silence. The den of a monk. His bed was dotted with tarry black, as if a rain of stars had fallen on his mattress and burned it.

I started out in life with a big handicap. My cat mother had put five kittens into the world the first time she gave birth. Of my paterfamilias, not a trace. I know nothing about him and it's probably better that way. Looking for a father is a trail that takes you nowhere, like a vinyl record turning round and round.

Of my mother, I now a bit more. I just had the time to understand that she was a good mother, as loving and devoted as a hoopoe. Our relationship was suddenly broken by an implacable hand.

There was, in that house, a woman with a back more bowed than a tree bending under the snow. One day, this very pious woman took care of drowning four out of the five kittens of the household. My bewildered mother was running all over the house, her neurons buzzing and jumping like popcorn. Suddenly, the old puritan woman turned to me with a mad eye and drool on her lips. She tried to catch me in my turn by the scruff of the neck but I inexplicably succeeded in jumping out the window of the kitchen that gave onto J. Edgar Hoover Street.

I am the only survivor of my family.

Numb with fear, drenched in sweat, unable either to run away from that house or throw myself into the lion's den, I remained in the middle of the street for an eternity. I barely escaped the tires of three or four cars. The drivers managed to brake or avoid me at the very last minute; luckily, I was on a one-way road going uphill.

And then a gray cat came to save me. Without unclenching his teeth, my savior pulled me by the paw. I followed him docilely.

I didn't have an ounce of energy left. I was deaf and dumb, the horns reached my ears, but didn't reach my cerebral cortex. As I think about it, at that moment I think I wanted to die. And then a warning shot from my savior's lips:

"Don't do anything stupid!"

These four words saved me. I followed the order. That's how I met Shasha, a female Abyssinian kitten and an orphan like me.

Although relatively younger, Shasha was streetwise. She shook out my fleas, dried my tears and opened her heart. I adopted her on the spot.

That's how she was, my little sister Shasha. A ball of instinct. In turn, I behaved like a big brother. I acted that way. I took her under my wing, that creature who, as a game or out of mischievousness, took herself for a female dragon and loved to play her favorite game: spitting fire. As far as I know, Shasha never managed to spit fire and her little tail was more like a little piggy's than a dragon's tail.

I extirpated Shasha from the claws of that accursed city where misfortune jumps from household to household with the punctuality of fate. Sometimes I felt bad and yet I knew you never go back over the traces of your past. My world was dead. I had to flee and give up everything, even my memories.

Of course, I never saw my brothers and sister again. Nor my mother, who was the first to suffocate in the chlorinated, soapy water.

I abhor Brooklyn. Never again will that transit city see the tip of my nose. And yet so far, my circus-like life has only been a series of stopovers. Travels, baggage, a succession of hotel rooms. In short, a life of wandering, with no time to build friendships and the few friends you manage to make, you only see them occasionally.

What about Shasha, where can she be now? Somewhere in the belly of Manhattan? I really miss her. She's the most playful, inoffensive kitten I know.

I remember her little face, the invisible sign she has above her nose, the dark marking that separates her cabbage-leaf-shaped ears, her big black eyes and thick lashes that veil the surface of her eyes. I'd give anything to see Shasha again with her head burrowing into a dry bramble bush, her downy tail keeping time like a conductor's baton. The features of her face are imprinted on my retina. I will try to find her as soon as we leave Paris.

Occupy New York

Of course a camel can't pass through the eye of a needle nor can a zebra ride horseback, and yet I have seen small miracles happen with my own eyes. I have seen beggars arise and march on the temple of money, towards Park Avenue. And I have seen my affectionate friend and master regain his smile. As the years go by, it seems that Sammy has succeeded in silencing everything around him and consequently around me, too. He's often tired. Melancholy. With drooping eyelids, his chin on his chest, he looks like he has withdrawn into his thoughts again. Like he has slipped effortlessly into the folds of the universe. He's far away, out of reach.

One night, I was awakened by an imperceptible little noise. On velvet paws, I crept into his room without making a sound. Sammy was stretched out, with his right leg folded along his left, resting against the wall. His eyes were moist. His forehead, burning. His lips, while dry, were the color of beet juice. He was breathing deeply, like a baby who'd cried all day. A heavy silence had fallen in the apartment as if the walls wanted to catch the breath of the world, smothering the rest—the blowing of the wind, the crash of thunder or the explosions of the volcanoes at the other end of the world. In the sealed case of this thick silence, in the den of this splendid chaos, the dazzling flash of Life shot upwards, thousands of years ago. Music is its other name.

Some biographers claim you can measure the importance of an artist by the power of his admirers or the fortune of his patrons. It was true in the past, in the time of kings and princes who protected performers. It's a lot more uncertain now that foundations have turned philanthropic and sponsorship has become a machine to deflate their tax returns.

I inspect his room, with one eye glued to the becalmed face of the performer. The old poster of Muhammad Ali is right there still, tacked onto the front door. A red, half-empty pack of Marlboros is lying under the bed. A jazz dictionary teeters on the little African table; it was written by a team of scholars from Columbia University, which is a few blocks away from our apartment. No mention of Sammy. Not even an allusion in a footnote. Jazz critics consider him a blues player, blues specialists classify him as a jazz musician. For poets, he remains first and foremost a musician, and for musicians he is recognized as an authentic poet. True, in his interviews, Sammy contradicted neither and let the pedants jabber away instead.

Being with Sammy isn't always easy. In restaurants, he is frugal, nibbling half-heartedly while holding forth about the scandalous policies of George W. Bush or the programmed suicide of his community: the Blacks, or as they say today, the African Americans who saw one of their own lift himself up to the presidency. Sammy may not live long enough to enjoy what seemed a fairy-tale even to the most optimistic of them.

He's all tense, worried and worrying. An inner fire burns constantly in him. He's always angry, getting on his high horse for nothing, for a subway train he missed or a wet cigarette that refuses the flame of the lighter. He does nothing, like everyone else. He says nothing about the passing of time or the weather, the predicted snowfall or the spring that will turn buds into flowers.

A man like that never gives you time to breathe. People fear him, shun him. He's rapidly becoming someone you don't want to associate with. It's a pity people judge by appearances. Under Sammy's armor, there beats a big, trembling heart. On one rainy, melan-choly day, in one of those books lying around in the bathroom of our apartment, I found a poem that com-forted me. I remember the strange name of its author, strange at least to my New York cat's ears. Abdellatif Laâbi, that's his name all right, and I imagine him as a wise old sage who has seen many doors open and close. I'll recite it for you from memory:

O gardener of the soul
have you foreseen
a plot of human earth
where you can still plant a few dreams?
Have you picked out the grains
brightened up the tools
consulted the flight of birds

observed the stars, the faces
the pebbles and the waves?
Has love spoken to you these days
in its foreign tongue?
Have you lit another candle
to wound the night in its pride?
Do speak up
if you're still here
At least tell me
what did you eat and what did you drink?

Hey Sammy, what did you eat and drink for the past few days? Your musicians don't hang out with you as in the good old days. Once the concert's over, everybody goes their own way, some jumping into their train for New Jersey, others going back to their house in upstate New York by car. You're in a bad mood and decide to take a cab. You don't feel like getting a breath of fresh air and using your long strides to get back to your apartment on Broadway and 105th Street.

Your real friends give you support from time to time, but avoid getting into conversations with you about topics dealing with black people or any other delicate subject that would make you mad.

Your family keeps quiet or vanishes. Your first wife cut off all contact with you. Sheila Jameela, your second wife, quickly learned to live with the situation and refused to cross swords with you. Distance is her best protection. From Los Angeles, she shudders at the idea of finding you on her doorstep again, unkempt and dirty, feverish, stinking of whisky. She saves her energy for the education of Princess Dahlia, to whom you—the Daddy of the rosy years, the happy years—dedicated *Eye to Eye*, the most tender and affectionate album I know.

Sheila is convinced of one thing. She trusts her intuition: if Sammy's genius is at all manageable, it's only at a distance. And I must admit she's completely right.

After *Eye to Eye* came out, your relationship grew looser. Not all at once. But by a series of imperceptible little jolts. You were then a proud, smug forty-year-old. You were at the height of your career, piling up the records, raking in successes. They'd predicted a truly enviable rise for you: you'd knock The Jackson Five, Stevie Wonder, and even James Brown—the hardest worker the American music industry has ever known—off their thrones. If you could only handle your career a bit better.

Second-hand testimony accumulates, but everyone agrees you're recklessly wasting your talent, and in an amazing way. What they say about you is that you're domineering and condescending, and that success inoculated you with the cancer of arrogance. You associate with gangsters, Italian Americans from New Jersey. Something deep inside you wants to go downwards again, something always pulls you toward the bottom. Your flame is at half-mast, your voice is harsher, and your diction pastier. The fans translate that last comment, full of innuendo, into quarts of cognac and cartons of Marlboro. Of course alcohol and tobacco aren't alone in the dock, they say, shaking their heads and muttering like kids caught with their hands in the cookie jar.

Those mean-spirited gossips are tenacious, relentless! They're never short of arguments and predictions. Some snarl that Curtis Mayfield was staying at the top of his career through sheer abnegation. Others point out that the effervescent Sly Stone calmed down a lot by following James Brown's advice to the letter. So why can't Sammy listen to his colleagues who've all gone through such great ordeals? Why can't their methods inspire him if he has no other solution to extricate himself from the shadow of evil? Why should he be an exception? How is he better than the other brothers? they conclude, their mouths full of spiteful pride.

From anecdote to piece of gossip, from rumor to slander, your bad reputation, Sammy, is spreading at dizzying speed on the marked trails of showbiz. At this rate, concert halls will be no more than a distant memory and little clubs will be fed up with your sudden changes of mood, that lack of professionalism that sticks to your skin like gum under the sole of your shoe.

If for some unknown reason one of your musicians defects, the destructive work of the rumor mill swings into motion again: it means the instrumentalists are afraid of going on tour with you, except maybe for the young pianist Kim Jordan, the junior of the band.

For me, things weren't looking any better, at least before I met the alchemist. I didn't think I could survive in the sewers of Manhattan, even with Shasha's support. Life expectancy there is a few weeks at the most.

Today the streets seem more dangerous than when Mayor Rudy Giuliani administered the megalopolis. And not just because the mobs have moved in a stone's throw from Wall Street and the rich people are at bay. The new mayor has declared war on the demonstrators, the homeless and stray animals. His mobile units show their muscle all over the city. You'd think the successor of Rudy Giuliani is playing *Apocalypse Now* again right in the middle of the Big Apple. If a few observers mocked his show of force at first, the media immediately got right behind Mr. Clean.

Large men and women in combat uniforms with full helmets on their heads, clubs in their hands, and revolvers at their hips stormed the nearby avenues. They endured the insults, the stones, and the bottles we hurled at them. They replied with tear gas and water cannon that got the better of our makeshift barricades. The boldest of us tried to stop the convoys of police vans and the deployment of foot soldiers. Girls from rich neighborhoods wearing pretty white bridal dresses came to support our desperate battle. Then it turned epic.

Holding hands, they burst into song, shouted, roared as if they were facing a cohort of white doves. Their idea was to decorate all the assault rifles with carnations. They were soon disillusioned.

Once the rabble was swept off the streets, the theater of operations moved to the periphery, following the wish of its director. The vagrants were taken where they came from, back to their cities blighted by violence and poverty like Baltimore and Camden, New Jersey. Legal advisers brought up all possible scenarios, weighing the pros and cons. From now on, everything was to be decided privately, behind closed doors, between lawyers and experts, under the marble and stucco of the tribunals. The sequences followed each other with a diabolical precision that would make the Pentagon jealous. Nothing resisted Giuliani's successor, who strutted around on television sets. The homeless didn't know which way to turn. The ones in Zuccotti Park, who showed more solidarity than the students from the Village, remained united and managed to push back the forces of repression.

A week later, Mr. Clean got a law passed that made it illegal to occupy any building, sewer, vacant lot, a section of the sidewalk, someone's mobile home or barge without authorization.

And so it was in the middle of the '90s when New York turned pale and white. Black people are no longer an important component of the city as they were in the past. It's the end of an era. And not only for minorities.

Under the assaults of music brokers and artistic directors, black music, the great electric current that vies with the Gulf Stream, is in crisis. Crack is devastating the black ghettos, throwing poor wretches with no home and no resources into the abyss. Homeless people of all ages congregate under bridges. They warm their hands over a brazier, scratching their mangy skin before slipping under a pile of cardboard boxes to disappear from the world. Gangs rip each other apart in interminable fights. New York is a monster without a mask, a greedy werewolf gobbling up the kittens of the family. All is not lost, for if the poor are invited to go graze elsewhere, their old neighborhoods are cleaned up, renovated, and resold to the little sharks of the new economy; the other sharks occupy Wall Street. Michael Bloomberg, the mayor, is quite proud of his new city. The Fulton Fish Market has had its day. Times Square can now welcome tourists in complete safety. The police are everywhere. Under the apparent calm, however, anger is seething, the beggars are not far off, and the machine is almost on the point of stalling.

My God, how sad New York is. Harlem has become bourgeois and drab. It's not only Harlem that changed. The people have changed, too, and in such a short time. Before, they wrote each other letters. They illustrated them with little drawings, affectionate words like "I LUV U" or things like that. Then they put them into envelopes, glued stamps into the little rectangle to the right and took the trouble to go to the post office to entrust their precious letters to the postman. Public phones were still used. People would stand on line in front of the booth, and while waiting, they counted and recounted the yellow coins they had to slip into the slot of the machine before tapping the numbers on the steel keyboard. Making a long-distance call wasn't just a formality but an act that created a social ritual.

At the dawn of the nineties, New York launched new objects that would soon become as familiar as the evening news. Email, the internet, the digital bubble, the virtual world. Preceded by a solid reputation, they arrived like conquerors. Adulated, coddled, hailed as miracle panaceas, they have burrowed into the folds of our daily lives. They have clasped us in their magic wires; if they let go of us it's only to attract us again. You'd think they had been around since the beginning of the first song of the world.

It's at the end of the last sequence, after the situation got totally out of control that I finally understood nothing would be the way it was before, when I was an alley cat. I understood that in New York, there is now a Before and an After Rudy Giuliani. I decided to leave the street. I didn't have the strength for this kind of life anymore and still less the desire. All the more so as I was certain that in a few days the poor, the sick, and the homeless would only be a bad dream, stirring at the borders of remorse. A bad dream to wipe away with a blink of my eyelids.

At that time, I was as badly off as Sammy the rebel who was now without illusions or causes to fight for. I was skinny as a rail, dirty, and insomniac. I was beginning to scare children and the weird creatures I sometimes ran into. I scratched myself all the time: fleas and vermin swarmed under my rough coat. At night, when death and fear come perform their sinister dance in the theater of the city, you had to be doubly cautious.

Watch out for your neighbor. The poor spend their time devouring each other, thus making the work of the police easier. The cats of Harlem know that a black kid has a hundred more chances to find himself behind bars than in college. They know that most of the victims know their executioners or their rapists, often a parent or a neighbor. And they know the poor tear their brothers to pieces before attacking a distant enemy.

After the assassination of Moses, the bum in Washington Square who kept chicken bones he picked out of garbage cans for Shasha and me, the course of our existence took on a new turn. The day after Mr. Clean's decree, we cried our eyes out for poor Moses, then we prayed for his soul and finally we shook off our fleas before trying to get on line for the soup kitchen in Union Square. The long line wasn't moving. New beggars—some agitated, others spaced out—planted themselves at the head of the line. People were pushing each other around and blows were flying. Victims fell down. And of course, when we finally made it through, the pots were empty. Shasha and I said resolutely: "This time we're going to earn our bread another way!"

From that day on, we were no longer the same flea-ridden cats, whining over their fate and sweating with fear. We were transformed, like the salamanders of ancient religions. Suddenly I had a new coat of fur and the tail of a young, active dragon. I was beginning a new life and the rejuvenated Shasha went her own way.

It was written in the great book of blues that we would survive in Manhattan with or without Michael Bloomberg, Rudolph Giuliani's successor in the mayor's office since January 1, 2002. We had the rage born of despair and the "everything is possible" culture that Moses had the time to instill in us. Nobody could break down our determination. It was time to turn the page and move on.

The Fatherless Son

Born on April 1st. No, that's not a joke. Maybe one of those rolls of the dice the stars are familiar with—unless it's a magic trick performed by the mysterious Papa Legba. In any case, Sammy really was born April 1, 1949 in South Chicago, in the state of Illinois. At the other end of the planet, in the middle of a sacred forest in Africa (or was it Cuba?), an old black man with a luminous face burst into a gravelly laugh that shook the mountains and made the ground dance like water in a brook. From his bamboo flute, a pure, crystalline sound burst forth, ricocheting against all the trees of the forest. The echo of the flute alerted a matronly woman standing at the doorstep of her hut. While pouring a little white rum on the laterite, this inhabitant of the area around Salvador de Bahia invoked the protection of the ancestors for little Samuel, born to Roberta Williams (Bobbie, to avoid any confusion about the gender of the mother, who was named that way in honor of her own father) and Reginald Kamau, a soccer player born in Jamaica. At the exact same time, in the early morning hours, lightning struck a little village in Louisiana, waking up the dogs who began barking in unison. In Washington, it rained cats and dogs; the tumultuous waters of the Potomac ripped open the pedestrian streets downtown, carrying away everything in their path. In Chicago, a mother was changing her first baby who'd been crying like a little blue devil all through the day of April 1, 1949.

Bobbie is overjoyed and her heart is dancing. She has eyes only for her chubby baby. She caresses him affectionately, massaging his fragile head and avoiding the fontanelle from which, who knows? the soul of the infant might escape. She licks his silky skin with feline application. Light and regal, she often purses her lips as if she wanted to blow on a spoon of boiling hot milk. She feels fulfilled in every fiber of her body, even if her nervous system is hardly resting. Something is bothering her but she doesn't know what.

The two men of her life are a gift from the heavens. The first is nice and warm in her muscular arms. The second attracts ecstatic or envious glances. She's doesn't dread the diapers to wash, the porridge to heat up, the wash to do, and the bath to give. She does it all alone, and besides, Reginald usually takes off.

Men are afraid of women. It's a fear—I know this instinctively—that comes to them from as far away as the gift of life. It's probably this fear that's going to drive Reginald Kamau away from his family.

In the street, the guy doesn't go unnoticed. Girls turn around as he passes. He walks with a jumpy, elastic step. The bulging muscles of his posterior are the object of lewd comments. He dresses tastefully, showing off his biceps and his torso, hugged in a white T-shirt, the latest rage. It's an accessory that soldiers originally wore under their combat uniforms. Marlon Brando and James Dean made it popular and the young black men returning from the European battlefields had no intention of leaving this bit of cloth to the white icons lounging around the pools of Beverly Hills while they had to face Nazi fire from one day to the next.

While my future preceptor has not yet blown out his second candle, Reginald Kamau can be found as early as the fall of 1951 in the main soccer club of Detroit, the city of the automobile and the cradle of northern blues.

It was very cold that year. The vacant lots are frozen. As they walk down the sidelines, people breathe out clouds of icy steam. But the Jamaican is the one who bears on his broad shoulders the potential offensive line of the Corinthians. A strange life trajectory for this man who came out of nothingness, a man lucky and mischievous as few humans can be.

Fleeing poverty, he came to Chicago at the age of fifteen or sixteen. He arrived in a rusty freighter from Kingston with an obligatory stopover in the Bahamas. His family never had the means to feed seven bawling, healthy children. He has the look of a boxer, but beneath his tough looks lies the beating heart of a dreamer. By a twist of fate, he chose America. And yet in his childish, fearful imagination, many other names were resonating in his ear, names that went far, sliding along the magical boulevards of this vast world.

Two years later, he can be found in a factory that produces cheap electricity. He has a passion for sport: with his co-workers, he kicks a ball around a field belonging to Western Electric. The Chicago Maroons, the local soccer club, call for his services before reluctantly letting him go to the semi-professional Detroit Corinthians.

The rumor goes around that a bumpkin from Jamaica, strong as an Andalusian bull, performs magic with a leather ball. Headhunters prowl around the stadium, looking for the special gem. In the pond next to the stadium, the tall grass begins to whir as soon as Reginald Kamau scores a new goal. The frogs hop from water lily to water lily in a silence disturbed only by a slight splash. Bees flit from bush to bush gleaning pollen. Large, soot-colored clouds move across the sky. A storm looms ahead.

Once on the field, Reginald is a prince. When he has a ball at his feet, he is unreachable. He could have been a sprinter or a boxer. He's equally impressive in track and field. He's the king, in any sport.

Passion and talent attract lightning. And lightning attracts sharks. The negotiations don't take long. The headhunters are happy. Their player is dazzled by so much consideration, so much attention to his person, which had remained in the shadows until now. Carried away by success, Reginald inexorably moves away, turning his back on his family. That's how men are: they often forget what is essential and blow, unknowingly, on the embers which will start great fires tomorrow. The Caribbean man is a son of exile. He leaves, comes back and sails off again with the wind. Although I didn't know him personally, his traces are visible everywhere. A smile from Sammy and I can see Reginald, or his ghost. And his presence or absence calls in dreams, visions and stories, whether or not they're connected to his legendary career. Stories, ancient or recent, which put a soothing salve on the wounds of yesterday and of today.

"A fool had a coffer full of gold, which he left behind when he died. A year later, his son saw him in a dream in the shape of a gray mouse with eyes full of tearss, prowling around the spot where his gold was buried. His son said he'd questioned him, saying: 'Why did you come here, tell me?'

"The father answered: 'I hid gold here and I came to see if anyone discovered it.'

"The son asked him: 'But why did you take on the shape of a mouse?'

"He said: 'Son, the heart in which the love of gold has arisen takes on this shape. Look at me carefully and profit from what you see by giving up gold, my child.'"

Reginald goes off alone again, leaving his family in Illinois. The agents have done the groundwork for him. The big leap does not frighten him and the oceans do not put him off. Reginald is now playing center forward in the professional team of the Glasgow Celtic, in Scotland.

Reginald is living in a hotel in the middle of Glasgow. While he does train a lot, he spends most of his time listening to the latest records imported from America. He finds them in Lewis & Sons, a record store with a keen interest in black music.

My real life began in the fog and meadows of Scotland, he'll say later. This makes him popular with sportswriters. In Jamaica, Reginald comes from a long line of vagabonds, sailors, and preachers. As a child, he had dreamed of the cities where his grandparents, uncles, and cousins had settled, in Cuba, Panama, or New Orleans. In each of these countries, it is said that they made fortunes, founded dynasties, ran companies, and led churches. And everywhere, in Venezuela as elsewhere, they went through ruin, wars, and revolutions. Most of them lost everything but their traces are vibrant with that inexhaustible energy that goes from generation to generation as the toad jumps hops from water lily to water lily.

A descendant of a modest branch of the family, Reginald is still proud of the family legend. He builds his own on the grass by scoring the victory goal in his very first game with those Celtic devils. A star is born. His photo circulates around the kingdom. This renown gives off a perfume of faraway places, a smell of black Caribbean exoticism. Something extraordinary, as fog in the bay of London but a fog ripped away to reveal a Spanish galleon.

In two seasons, Reginald Kamau, nicknamed the Black Arrow, stuns the Scottish fans with his dribbles, accelerations, jokes, generosity, and pleasant temperament. He enters history as the first player of color in the First Division championship of the United Kingdom. And opens the way for a battalion of players from the Windward Islands, Barbados, Saint-Kitts-and-Nevis, Trinidad and Tobago, and from his own native island.

All is not rosy in the young career of the Jamaican. Tired of the brutality of the British way of playing and the vulgar, racist shouts—cries of the jungle right out of *Tarzan*—coming at him from the fringe of the crowd, he suddenly ends his contract. Considering that life is movement, that no empire is eternal, no fortune permanently acquired, did he give his decision much thought? Or was he acting on impulse? No one will ever know, not even his agent. He returns to Detroit in 1954 after three remarkable seasons.

Bobbie is not there to welcome him. Their relationship shattered a long time ago. Reginald would not see his Sammy again before he was eight. Meanwhile, Bobbie accepted a position as an English teacher in a high school in Puerto Rico, an American colony in the Caribbean. His mother went off alone too, so Sammy was entrusted to his grandmother, Lily Williams, who has always lived in Savannah, Tennessee. Bobbie plans to get her son back as soon as things settle down a bit. Sammy had just blown out his second candle on Lily Williams' lap.

"I feel different on the field," Reginald says.

Nobody pays attention to his words. His teammates pass each other the ball, this one tries to shoot a penalty goal, that one a corner, while the goalkeeper picks up his gloves and the coach chats with a player who's warming up along the sideline.

"I feel different." That's his mantra on the field. And off the fields. As if he wanted to contain his overflowing energy in the corset of practice and habit.

Alone and childless, Reginald is bored stiff in South Chicago, some say. Others, pettier and more spiteful, have put on paper the exact time and reasons for his trips to Detroit where his soccer club is located and don't shrink from sending treacherous little anonymous notes to Bobbie. Each new letter petrifies the young woman. For a long time, she believed that lasting happiness was hidden outside, behind a tree, like a rabbit. She saw the tip of its nose, she perceived its shadow, its mass, the quivers emanating from it. Now, she dreads opening those little well-sealed envelopes like the plague. They bear no address but never fail to reach her in Puerto Rico. She senses that she won't see her husband again unless there's a miracle: the intervention of the Angel of Consolation, the very same one who appeared to Christ in the Garden of Olives, could put Reginald back on the path to their home. Every morning, before drinking her coffee (unsweetened), she longs to take Reginald and Sammy in her arms but she embraces only shadows. Home is cut in two. Stillborn. Tensions from another time, the sequels of slavery and the heartbreaks of exile continue to affect people's lives. Like the aftershocks of an earthquake. No need to be a geologist to feel this palpable suffering written in the inheritance of clashes and struggles. As an adult, Sammy will apply himself to lighting these stigmata with the lantern of his voice, to naming these demons. Even when he's back in Chicago, his father can't imagine that one day his prodigy son will compose a song in honor of the black metropolis of Michigan. "We Almost Lost Detroit," a beautiful, somber requiem like a prophecy dedicated to the capital of the automobile hard hit by unemployment and relocation.

For the moment, Reginald parties, invites young people to his huge apartment. They scat and rock 'n' roll. They sing at the top of their voices, get high, and drink to quench an ancient thirst. They prefer pleasures, marijuana, liquor, and music to the austere temptation of posterity.

If I close my eyelids, I can imagine him in the company of his friends. I see him winding up his gramophone to listen over and over to the popular records: Cab Calloway, Fats Waller, and Louis Armstrong propel the hot-headed youth into the fourth dimension.

Be-bop-a-Lula
I wanna be loved by you.
Be-bop-a-Lula
I wanna be loved by you.

The old stringy-furred cat that I am still loves scat today. It owes everything to our family: the Felidae. Cab Calloway certainly knew how to imitate us when he launched his famous "The Hi Dee Ho Man." A wild cat gone astray among humans. He would dialogue with the band on a carpet of onomatopoeias, meows, and chuckles interspersed with high-pitched vocalizations.

On the dance floor or in the depths of his living room, Reginald is always surrounded by people. His travels and his terrific talent as a storyteller make him charismatic. He describes transatlantic crossings like a magic adventure and Scotland like a moss-green province of paradise. Whirling on the field, he never stays still. He's a dancing butterfly who attracts the light onto everything he touches. His impatience is legendary. With him, one rule only: it's everything—and *now*.

Everything or nothing.

The party won't last. His savings melt like snow. He has to go back to the factory, hire himself out as a welder, as an electrician, or work in a body shop, hammering and nailing away eight hours straight. The time to get back into financial health, then a new hope shines at the end of the tunnel. Nina would say the African gods are sometimes very kind. Those gods, with their perfectly shaped forms and their speech with subtly rhythmed repetitions accentuating its incantatory nature, help humans out more often than one might think. Apparently, they forgot the body-shop worker in shorts and spikes.

It is said that interaction with your fellow human beings is an indispensable experience. But for us felines, solitude is an essential, imperious need. During the summer of 1956, another headhunter crosses the path of the Black Arrow. He's Portuguese, a flatterer with a certain flair. He coddles Reginald, putting a manly arm around his shoulders, slipping delicious words in his ear.

"More than just a soccer player, Reginald is an idol. The hope of his people," he yaps to a sportswriter.

The agent has every intention of sending Reginald to the best destination possible, but he makes the pleasure last. Fifteen minutes later, he lays his cards on the table.

"With me by his side, he'll do great in a major club worthy of his rank."

A new silence.

Suspense.

"Reggie is expected at the football club of Porto, the FC Porto," he finally spits out.

The sportswriter is incredulous and looks at him wide-eyed. Then he rushes to wire the news. A few days later, the agent meets his protégé again but what do you know! No more FC Porto.

This agent is a number one bluffer.

"The Portuguese Consulate in Chicago's haggling over your visa. But listen, I wasted no time and found a new team for you."

Reginald says nothing, as if he weren't concerned at all. If, by some unlikely chance, a godsend fell into his lap, he'd accept it on the spot. This simple certainty had always allowed him to remain himself and keep a cool head. The wily agent doesn't give him the time to breathe. He calls him often, invites him out to eat, talks to him about this and that. Six weeks spent scheming and watching for signs. Fussing over him. Feeling his swimmer's shoulders to make sure the Jamaican is really his.

When the official announcement of his new destination finally reaches him, Reginald does not jump for joy. Breathing from the belly to control his cardiac rhythm, he gives the impression that nothing affects him. The next day, he dives right back into his routine: nights out, the dance floor, gambling, girls with burning eyes. And if someone asks him where he'll go next season, he declares that he has no idea. In short, he has only the vaguest idea of his future club. No matter, he's ready for adventure. His decision has been made a long time ago, and as always, on impulse.

One evening, his agent meets him at an upscale nightclub right near the Trap Door Theater with a bottle of champagne in his hand and a cigar between his lips, but the man he calls Reggie doesn't let himself be impressed. Between bursts of laughter and wreaths of cigarette smoke, he puts an end to the conversation and goes back to dancing scat with the girls with burning eyes and plump thighs.

The letters that come to him from San Juan, the capital of Puerto Rico swept by hurricanes, don't announce anything alarming. The baby's fine and so is the mother. Bobbie regularly gets news of Sammy. She calls Lily every week, always on Sunday morning before church. Being far away is hard on her, she cries a lot but in the end, she always chokes back her sorrow. She hardens herself. Promises to think of them, to pray for them. She also writes her mother every week, to pay the bills and take care of current business.

Reginald sees things differently, his ingenuousness strapped over his shoulder. According to him, she's the one who should communicate, give signs of life. The ones who stay behind contact the ones who've left, not vice-versa. What's more, children are just fine in the arms of women—big sisters, mothers, or grandmothers. It's women who bring them into the world and they're the ones who guide them and watch over them. Lily or Bobbie. Mother or grandmother, it boils down to the same thing. No need to go on about the mysteries of nature.

Contrary to people his age, Reginald never felt the need to program his life. Filling his life with family ambitions, keeping to a schedule, consolidating walls, and setting priorities is not for him. He lives as the wind takes him, with no plan and no illusions, as if he wanted to forget the world and let the world forget him. That's how he lived, in fair weather and in foul.

In the middle of May, an old steamer is cruising along the Florida coast, spitting out a long trail of smoke. Reginald Kamau, disoriented by the crossing, thinks he can recognize the steep cliffs of his childhood. He respectfully salutes the landscape filing past his moist eyes. He thinks he sees the enchanted hills of his native land. He hums a melancholy ballad in homage to the wooded, steep, and narrow valleys of his youth. That's how he finds himself in Brazil for one season.

The sun is there; it's the gold currency of the country. The Bay of All Saints off Bahia is unique in the world because of its visceral attachment to Africa. Imagine for a moment that you are, like Reginald Kamau, lost in the vast space of the Americas and you just fell upon a piece of Africa so vibrant it seems to contain all the sap and oxygen of the continent. So there's no room for doubt: you really are, body and soul, in Salvador de Bahia, at the very far east of that Brazil which shelters the largest black diaspora of the New World. That's where you are, enclosed in the solid wooden case of Africa.

The capital of the young state, Salvador de Bahia, is the place for all kinds of trafficking. African, European, and Native American cultures mingle to form a new human line the way sugarcane mixes with banana plants. A quarter of the population enslaved in the Americas transited through this port city, which also houses a significant colony of Persian cats brought over in the hold of ships to eradicate rats. Blacks arrived in waves. Extracted from the belly of the ship, piled up on the landings, offered to the customers who opened their mouths, slipped two fingers under their lip to check out their teeth and make sure they were in good health, and then sent out to work in the fields.

Strange, how Reginald Kamau feels in this black Brazil: he's like a fish in water. A proverb of his country comes to his mind: "Give him a pencil and a child will build his house."

He feels he's inside the skin of that child busy building the house of his dreams. Never, since he left his native island, has he felt such inner peace. His body seems to be perfectly molded into the red clay of Salvador. His steps don't stumble on the disjointed paving stones of the old city—no, they slide nonchalantly along. Reginald is floating on a very soft cloud.

The postcards he sends to his Detroit friends describe this city in magnificent, somewhat melodramatic, biblical terms. He compares Bahia to Jericho, with black drums instead of the trumpets that made the waters of the Jordan River rise.

Close your eyes now like Reginald Kamau in the great João de Bonfim cathedral, unfold an imaginary map in front of you and go back in time. Having left the third-largest city in Brazil, you're now on an African beach again, somewhere in Yoruba country or around Pointe-Noire in the Congo, and you'll find men and women exactly like the ones Reginald Kamau rubbed shoulders with on the wooded hills that saw him grow up.

During the day, he trains in the brand-new stadium. In the afternoon, he takes the obligatory nap. And at night, he dances the samba in the Pelourinho, the old center of town, on the square where the slave market used to be. The slaves never deserted this shore. They camp on the place of their afflictions.

Every cat knows that in Bahia, the Orishas, the divinities who left the African coasts, live out in the open, right in the midst of everybody. They are celebrated all day and all night long in the joyful fountain of youth, and not only by the artists and carnival dancers. The voices of common people resound in your ears long after the old toothless singer has stopped singing the last chorus of his praise of the divinity Shango or his acolyte Yemanja.

Reginald Kamau feels what the words "emotion," "fusion," or "effusion" mean in Salvador. Bahia is the pulsing heart of Africa. He goes from one group to another. An old man gives him an affectionate hug. The old singer concedes, between two bursts of laughter that reveal his black stumps, that he has a filial, carnal, deep relationship with the rites of candomblé. He raises a little the veil that hides the dress codes, the corporal inflections, the postures and the other signs of recognition unknown to the passing visitor. In his company, Reginald Kamau experiences a celebration of the senses. And all the buildings, all the rich or wretched houses, all the communal land, the suburbios, the theaters, the blocos, the terreiros, the casas, and the favelas, all the streets and narrow valleys—it all reminds him, stealthily if not openly, of the presence of the spirits who left centuries ago in the dark holds of the slave ships. And if he got the odd idea—not so odd really, given the spiritual context—of asking the *chuva*, the rain that's been falling hard since he arrived in Salvador de Bahia, the place where the chuva gets its vigor, it would unhesitatingly tell him that it is also, of course, in cahoots with the Orishas. That's how the African divinities take their revenge on the history of men. That's how their voices arise from the crowd of countless samba and carnival troupes. Those voices of yesteryear come twirling above the sacred woods that surround Salvador's Bay of All Saints where six-story buildings have been built, with no Blacks allowed. By their insolent luxury, they try to make you believe that modern Brazil has no reason to be jealous of the skyscrapers of New York or Chicago.

We think we choose our lives, but it's the other way around: it's life that chooses us. Life holds us in its net. Here you are deep into a life path, a story. Anchored to this base by your genes and your saliva, by your experience and what you have inherited from your ancestors. That force is huge, irresistible, but Reginald Kamau doesn't know that yet. From this point of view, there is no chance, no determinism, no entirely gratuitous act. He doesn't have much leeway and that's what gives his life its taste, that's what makes him both great and miserable.

Reginald's destiny on his Brazilian soccer field resembles a hot-air balloon driven by warm winds. A balloon free in its movements, at least so it seems. Reginald is unable to change its speed and direction. His destiny may be playing out in the air, but he has his feet in the mud and his ankles reddened by all kinds of servitude. He runs over the field like a tree looking for leaves.

Reginald is very much like that plant in the Sahara which consumes all its sap and energy in one day. As soon as the seed gets water, it begins to bud and then becomes a stem and grows leaves. And it produces a flower and seeds before it withers, and bingo! it's nighttime and it's all over.

Before he withers in one night, he takes his work as a soccer player seriously. After all, it's more fun than being an auto body worker at General Motors and the pay is better. Thank God his contract and visa were renewed by the local authorities, influenced by the boldness of the Portuguese agent—unless it was by the thickness of his wallet.

Nothing predestined this hairy Jamaican to become the Brazilian champion with the Red and Blue of the Esporte Clube Bahia in 1959. Brazil produces soccer players by the dozen. Nothing, except perhaps the hand of an indulgent God or the hand of a charming Devil. As for me, Paris, I'd be tempted to look for the finger-prints of Papa Legba on that lucky twist of fate.

As soon as Reginald Kamau arrives in 1956, the Esporte Clube wins the regional championship. He's not on the roster, he's sitting in the stands. But in 1958 he was definitely there to lift the same cup. O Cubano, as his team calls him, was decisive in winning the Brazilian Cup for them the next year.

On the field, harmony is perfect. Nadinho, Leone, Henrique, Flávio, Vicente, Beto, Agachados, Marito, Alencar, Bombeiro, and Biriba welcome him like a brother. Reginald loves their game, all short passes and technical wonders. Keeping the ball as long as possible— that's the secret of the Bahians' style. They play soccer as if they were on their way to a dance or to church. Two words can characterize the way they play: explosion and creativity. Nothing to do with the long rushes at the goalie, the ABC of the Glasgow Celtic's game.

Outside the stadium, Reginald is well integrated. At the end of a game, the players are surrounded by a swarm of girls with generous hips and a glass of cachaça in their hands. And the amazons take them by the shoulders. Give them loud, ardent kisses on the lips while wriggling their bellies. The nights are long, humid, and lively. Bahia is red as the setting sun. It's not just the sex. It's not just the delicious, spicy, fragrant dishes and the cocktails with a base of *maracuja, morango, caju,* or *abacaxi.* It's not just the practice on the secondary playing field of Almaviva. It's all the rest, too. Dream and reality mixed together. Grace and beauty. Feet that never leave contact with the ground, eyes that are never raised to the ineffable heavens. When night falls, the flash of another world erases the dull routine of the ball rolling over the muddy ground of the soccer field. A world high in color and relief offers itself to him. The moist, warm satin of skins embracing each other. The cascades of laughter. The flow of tenderness. The ecstasy of pleasure. The flowers of the night, now birds, now butterflies. And everywhere life rising and beating time. The Divine Song.

In Bahia, Reginald Kamau attends the festivities of July 2, 1958 on Pelourinho Square. In the humid, intoxicating heat of Bahia they are celebrating, before his eyes, the birth of the independence of Brazil on July 2, 1823. In the early hours of morning, he saw a human mass storm the old, narrow streets of the Pelourinho—the historic center of the city—and head toward the big square. Brass bands, parades, processions, banners. Music and dancing at every stop and often every two yards. T-shirts in the colors of the country, with yellow dominating. Faces garishly painted. Laughter, joy, the unhinging of the senses. You can't say no to the African divinities who've taken on human shape. *Alegria, alegria,*

alegria. People hug him, kiss him. Now he's lost in the Pelourinho, carried away by the immense crowd.

Reginald Kamau changed in his very first season. He got thinner, he's sharper on the field, but there's more. His gestures have changed, the way he walks is lighter. When he runs, he seems to flow, or more precisely, his flesh, his bones and his muscles are flowing out into the Brazilian air.

He doesn't see things in the same way anymore. The metamorphosis started when he arrived in Bahia, a city with three hundred and sixty-five Catholic churches with solid gold altars, but he didn't notice anything. It began quite slowly, unbeknownst to him. First there were eyes staring at him. Not languorously but on the contrary an enveloping, blazing attention that gives you the feeling that all these stingers are snatching you up, infiltrating you, and there's nothing you can do about it.

He also saw with his own eyes the customs of the Blacks of Brazil. Men and women all dressed in white, drinking and eating, praying and honoring the spirits of their ancestors, dancing and singing for them. Nothing had prepared him for that. And he saw other things that seemed still stranger at first but finally not so strange, for they later become so sweet and natural. The leaping priestesses, the blood clotted on the relics, the thundering drums, the interminable trances, the fires lit in the concessions. The offerings to the Orishas. The dancers, turning, and twirling, crawling, dusting themselves off, growling, and flying away. Dying to be reborn again. Yes, he saw all these creatures close up. He approached them without asking for anything in return. He let them come to him like a calabash gliding over the water. Trusting his inner ear, he let himself get carried away by all that drama. Without resisting or trying to understand the ancient rites, the obligatory figures, the gestures and secret codes.

He attended these ceremonies again and again, as a spectator attracted by some underground force. Nothing and nobody had prepared him for such a discovery. Week after week, he would come back from them relieved of his soccer worries, with his muscles unknotted, his joints rested. At peace, lighter, he would open one after the other the doors and the windows overlooking the myths and rites of the new world he'd caught a glimpse of as he watched this liturgical choreography of a new kind.

Reginald feels liberated, relieved of a burden, of a remorse. Of a curse. The curse that hangs over the heads of the young Blacks born in Jamaica, Chicago, or elsewhere in the United States.

The Brilliant Student

New York and its legend now. Its strange, tenacious roots burrow deep inside the imagination. The city resounds with a thousand languages in an uninterrupted panting of men and machines. Rich in long asphalted thoroughfares, sparkling skyscrapers, and lonely crowds, this port city is poor in love and compassion. At least, that's how its inhabitants see it.

At the age of thirteen, Sammy is in New York with his mother. She feels like a stranger to him. He spent the first twelve years of his life in his grandmother's arms and has a limitless, unconditional affection for her. The little hick straight from Savannah, Tennessee, discovers the metropolis. He's bewildered. He huddles up to Bobbie. He's also cold. The very first night, she gives him sage tea to warm him up.

Bobbie has found public housing in Chelsea, a mainly Puerto Rican neighborhood, on West Eighteenth Street. There are no Blacks there except for this little single-parent family. The apartments are new, narrow, and hospital clean. The rent, reasonable for the time.

Exile and solitude, a familiar feeling. They soon get used to living together. They'll have all the time in the world to get to know each other. Bobbie found a job as a librarian and Sammy a good middle school, thanks to his good grades.

He's accepted at DeWitt Clinton in the Bronx, a school with an excellent reputation. He goes there every day without Bobbie, who has left at dawn. You must appreciate each day as if it were your first, Bobbie repeats. Sammy nods. Tries. And it works for him. He's a gentle, obedient boy with a smiling face. Everyone agrees that he works diligently and gets excellent grades. He likes reading, poetry, basketball. He towers over everybody. He's personable, considerate and always ready to help.

In the course of the last year, his English teacher, impressed by the quality of his compositions, moves heaven and earth to get him a scholarship to Fieldston, a private school generally reserved for the child prodigies of upper middle-class Jews.

Mawlana used to tell us that the places where we loved and suffered—and above all where we thought and dreamed—the places we left with no hope of ever seeing them again, appear more beautiful in memory than they were in reality.

The future mage would certainly agree with my august mentor and swami.

He's the one who told me how, when he got out of DeWitt Clinton, he was admitted to Fieldston, the most prestigious prep school on the banks of the Hudson. Bobbie is elated that day. She can't hold back her tears when Sammy, in his already deep voice, tells her the good news. She thanks the Lord. She also warns her son that the sword of Damocles hangs over his head and at the slightest misdemeanor he'd be expelled. The rich won't give you a second chance, says Bobbie, choking back her tears. Sammy, too, is on the verge of tears. He promises she can count on him and he'll be an exemplary student.

The next day, he's in that red-brick school. Out of the one hundred students registered there, Sammy counts how many kinky heads of hair pass him by in the long, brightly lit halls. All in all, there are only five Blacks.

At home, Bobbie is a stern mother, very strict as far as education is concerned. She's also the perfect home-maker: everything is in its place, sparkling clean. The long trips in the subway, her work as a librarian, the death of her mother, and her forced single life haven't broken her good humor. She's dedicated to her son and surrounds him with all her love. She teaches him strict, precise rules that the teenager follows to the letter. Between prayers and lessons, he can relax playing bas-ketball at school. He practices his scales at home every evening. But it's out of the question to linger in the street or hang out with anyone at all.

Fieldston is a bastion of liberalism. Only wealthy people can indulge in being liberals. It must be a passing fancy. How can they vote Democrat, for example, and advocate less taxes and individual freedom?

When classes are over, the students return to their fancy neighborhoods toward the Upper West Side. Sammy rushes out so as not to miss the subway, arrive late in Chelsea and get scolded by his mother.

Only one other student takes the same way home. His name is Paul Margot and he comes from a well-off Jewish family. Paul and Sammy are close, so much so that Bobbie permits her son to sleep over at the Margots once or twice a month.

Sammy really likes the Margot family. So does his mother. She rarely sees them but instinctively knows the five members of the tribe are good people.

As he never had the warm affection of a father, Sammy feels surges of tenderness for Jerry, his friend's dad. Jerry and Sammy love to talk politics. Although he's a conservative, Jerry is fascinated by utopian currents of thought. His politics are a mix of fierce anti-communism mixed with anarchism. Sammy has a political maturity remarkable for his age. His heart leans to the left. In any case, he's clearly more left-wing than Jerry.

Everything has been said about Sammy Kamau-Williams' childhood, including things no one knew. To recount it, old acquaintances sometimes turned into providential angels, that is, into very talkative storytellers. Paul Margot isn't like that. He's a man with principles, a faithful friend.

Paul Margot still remembers the feverish nights when his father and his best friend argued without stopping. He didn't forget how Sammy developed his arguments, calmly and firmly, how he wanted to re-examine everything and was for a socialism deliberately accepted by one and all. Jerry didn't share the opinions of his young fourteen-year-old opponent but he felt a mix of admiration and affection for him. Every other week, Sammy would sleep over at the Margots. Jerry lent him novels by Ayn Rand, an atheist, individualist, libertarian philosopher born in Russia under the name Alissa Zinovievna Rosenbaum. She was to inspire Ronald Reagan and the school of rational economics.

Sammy isn't impressed by the theses of the author of *We, The Living*, who is extremely popular. He annotates her works and systematically takes apart her arguments.

In 1963, when Sammy is fourteen and a half, he has a bull's neck and down on his chin. He has a smiling face and is a head taller than everybody else. He likes to laugh and make people laugh. He has a lot of fun on the athletic fields. The only odd trait that Paul Margot still remembers is his voice. Deep. Between tenor and bass. Later, Ron Carter—the bass virtuoso sought after by every jazz band—will say it was a voice to serve Shakespeare.

For sensitive, complicated people like Sammy, their childhood years are twice as important as they are for others. Everything comes to them from that childhood kingdom with its splashes of ochre and mud. When I was younger, I was a great hunter of lizards. I would break into a sprint just for the thrill of the hunt, to get a shot of adrenaline. Of course I never tasted the elastic flesh of those little reptiles but I loved to frighten them. As soon as a gecko became my prisoner, I would immediately let it go so as not to be tempted to tear it apart. First of all, every living creature is sacred. Animate and inanimate beings alike. And then, no one is immune from an impulsive reaction, lashing out with your claws for instance.

Like me, Sammy was a playful little boy. At the age of three, his little face flushed with an exuberant joy like a little elf, he would come up with rather strange questions. More than once, he asked his grandmother: "Is the rain happy to be outside, Granma?"

Lily Williams dreaded the questions that bothered her gifted grandson. For beneath his angelically peaceful appearance, Sammy is already tormented. He always feels hunted, spied on, watched. Always watchful, always in search of fresh air. He looks everywhere for his shadow, the twin brother he dreams of on certain nights. He knows that the two-headed vulture is never far off, that the woods of Savannah harbor a thousand beasts and death is prowling around.

Sammy's quest reminds me of a Persian or Turkish story. Perhaps you know the story of the donkey that fell into a well?

"There was a very old donkey who was no longer very useful, so old and worn-out was he. One day, he inadvertently fell to the bottom of a dried-up well in the yard of the farm where he'd lived ever since he was born. The farmer told himself that since he couldn't use the donkey and the well anymore, he would fill up the well, thus killing two birds with one stone. With his tow-truck and his tractor, he collected several cubic meters of earth. He invited his neighbors to a barbecue and then, at the end of the meal, he gave each of them a shovel and they set out to fill up the well.

"When they looked down the well to check the level of earth they had thrown in, they saw, to their surprise, that the donkey was still there and instead of being covered with earth, he was coming back up and would soon be out of the well. The donkey had taken advantage of the shovelfuls of earth, stamping them down as they arrived, to get back into the open air."

If Sammy can beat the forces pulling him down, I'm absolutely sure he'll regain the open air, too. And I'll be the happiest of cats. I will, thank God, consider my seventh life as one of the most fulfilled.

Before he's able to walk all the way up and relegate his fears into the closet of childhood, he'll let off steam, sometimes in sports and sometimes in music, in order to keep a level head.

At school, Sammy's whole life centers on sports. Basketball. Baseball. Football. On the playing fields, his sardonic smile never leaves him. He was the friendliest person and the most faithful friend, Paul Margot remembers again, quite excited at the idea of conversing with a philosophical cat. Lost in the woods of his past, he smiles mechanically, as if he wanted to display his little symmetrical teeth, perfectly aligned, like the two scales of Justice.

It's in English that Paul realizes for the first time that Sammy is much more than a charming boy. One day, the teacher asked all his students to write a personal composition, an authentic piece of life. A week later, the students are putting three pages of clichés annotated by the kindly hand of their teacher away in their bags when Sammy raises his hand and asks to read his composition. The teacher reacts to the student's audacity with a mischievous smile.

Everything stops immediately. Nothing stirs in the class. The forty pages go by, giving flesh to the little village of Savannah, Tennessee, where Sammy grew up. Everything has gone into it: the magic of the long evenings with people gathered together to sing and tell stories, the deep voice of the black people that had long been smothered by puritanical America, and even the magical hands of Lily. The tea made with sage, the sacred herb of the slaves in the cotton fields. Vivid descriptions. A precise sense of dialogue, profoundly warm, and no attempt to be funny just for the sake of being funny.

The bell rings. The students get up, silent and stunned. They've been transfigured. Icy tears are flowing down their cheeks. They leave Fieldston, walking across the big schoolyard with slow steps. From behind, you could sense they were in a kind of trance that would remain with them all night long.

In front of the gate, Paul manages to say thanks to Sammy. And this is the beginning of a long friendship.

Later, Sammy teaches Paul the piano and Paul teaches him to play the guitar. They found a little rock band with school friends: Paul on rhythmic guitar, Bill Horowitz on bass, David Appleby on drums and Ira Resnick, who sings hits by the Stones, the Beatles, and the Kinks. At the mike, Sammy takes turns with Ira in a tight black dress that gives her a deliberately vulgar look. Sammy sings his own compositions. He already knows what he's doing. He knows exactly what he wants. He's the life of the party. He doesn't shrink from slipping melodies taken from gospel into his texts. Even today, Paul Margot doesn't see a trace of mischief in it. Time has not altered the quality of his memories, rolled in tender feelings.

"Sammy was completely aware we came from very different social backgrounds. It was a blessing to have a friend like him in our midst!"

The band is invited to family parties, bar mitzvahs and birthdays. The Warlords are in demand, to blow a little breeze of madness into bourgeois living rooms, but the real warriors whose name the Fieldston kids adopted scour the shady bars of Greenwich Village. They hang out near the docks, the territory of dark, grubby hoods, of drug dealers with bushy eyebrows, sailors, the whores, and their pimps. And now there's a rumor during a jam session organized one evening in the student center of Manhattan College that the real Warlords have sneaked into the auditorium. Panic and chaos. Fear of violence. The hoods indifferently handle knives and baseball bats.

"I really think they really liked our music."

Forty-four years later, Paul Margot's eyes are twinkling. He hasn't forgotten a thing about this concert that could have turned into carnage.

What Bill Horowitz remembers most vividly from that period are the rehearsals. They always happen at his home in the wealthy suburb of Riverdale. Sammy arrives, says hello to everybody, then goes straight up to Nellie's room. Sammy plays cards for hours, his long legs stretched out on the carpet. His playing partner is none other than the youngest girl in the Horowitz family, ten years old.

When he finally agrees to leave Nellie, it's to jump on the little electric piano and play variations on his favorite song of the moment: "Go Now" by the British rock band The Moody Blues. Several versions of that weaving and unweaving the melodic lines of "Go Now" can still be heard. Once he's home again, he plays the same piece over and over until he knows the slightest pause in the melody. Bill recalls that Sammy sometimes deserted The Warlords to join another band from the same school. Did Sammy go there on his own to help out, or did he answer the appeal of Keith Kaufman, the leader of The Voodoo Buddies? To this day, no one knows for sure. Sammy goes from one group to another the way he goes from football to basketball, with the same ease and enjoyment.

Forty years later, David Schwartz, the math nerd from Fieldston, still appreciates Sammy's loyalty both in class and on the athletic fields.

"Sammy passed the ball, defended, scored points, and crossed the field in a few strides. He knew how to sweat for pleasure. His presence calmed us."

And David adds: "Sammy had a good word for everyone—including our worst enemies."

A high forehead, balding in a half-circle, pushing his curly hair out on the sides. Delicate features, a gentle and serene profile. The face of the bard Langston Hughes is part of Sammy's adolescence. We all need a hero to grow up and cross the coral reef of childhood more easily. I opted for Mawlana, my well of Sufi knowledge and wisdom. And Sammy, for the visionary poet.

Sammy discovers Langston Hughes on Lily's kitchen table in the pages of the *Chicago Defender*, the most popular newspaper of the black community. First, his portrait inside a medallion. Then those words, sentences, rhythm, and repetitions. He's hooked. The effect on him is instantaneous. Sammy, as if in apnea, devours the sublime poems and Hughes' weekly columns written quickly, with a stroke of his pen. Week after week, it's the same delight. More than a paternal figure, Langston Hughes is the goldsmith who turns iron into gold, the weaver of wonderful carpets where you breathe in the velvet of the moment. But there's something else, too: tact, lightness. For Sammy, all of Langston Hughes can be summed up in two words: pride and admiration. The little Tennessee kid had never felt that before.

In the image of his godfather, Sammy works at composing stories and poems with an elegance that is both precise and sober. He works a lot, taking inspiration from his piano lessons, alternating pleasure and effort. The results are rather positive. He makes his own formal harmonies, coupled with a genuine looseness that shows promise. Already Sammy wants to get out into the open and drink up the clouds. Unveil his future.

In 1967, Sammy is eighteen. Carefree as all prodigal sons are. He graduates from Fieldston. He has no intention of applying to Harvard, Yale, or Princeton. Comfort and security do not tempt him. He does nothing like other people. His friends at Fieldston take the royal road that has been marked out for them since they were born. Sammy has other dreams. He picks Lincoln, a small black college in the middle of Pennsylvania. The troubadour Langston Hughes went there before becoming the dandy of the Harlem Renaissance. Sammy can do no less than follow him; he feels armed for poetry. That's what he explains to Paul Margot.

Some people trace the main lines of their destiny on white paper, others etch them on soft wood. Since the dawn of time, gnawed by doubt and feeling his own twilight descending inside him, man has rebelled and, by the sheer force of his imagination, managed to push back what lives within darkness. As for me, I watch over my Sammy, who is hatching inside him a writer's temperament.

With my paws on the rudder, I'm at the helm, refining my guardian angel's agenda. I continue the task of protection that was performed years ago by an extraordinary little lady. You've already heard of her but you still don't know her very well. Her name was Lily. Lily Williams. She was the grandmother of Sammy Kamau-Williams. She knew how to probe her grandson's secret nooks and crannies like no one in the world. Like her, I can't allow myself to go on vacation, I cannot leave Sammy hanging between abyss and darkness for one single day.

Every morning, I give myself to a ritual whose details I will spare you. Let's just say that as soon as the sun rises, this ritual helps me to exercise a deep, subtle discernment. I let silence settle into my carnal envelope; I pay attention to my breathing. In complete awareness. Then I send my whole being into orbit, I simply point it in Sammy's direction. And wherever he may be on this earth, inside or outside the territory of the United States, I'm at his side or more exactly at his back. My soul sticks to his coattails. I hear his breath coming out of his throat in little jerky exhalations. I do not relax my attention. My breath superimposes itself on his. Gently. That's the way it's been since the beginning of our relationship. There's no reason for it to change.

I hate pets—dogs faithful to their owners, parrots who repeat bits of sentences over and over, kittens meowing by the fire. Everything about them puts me off, even the expression that puts man in the center and reduces us to the rank of a brainless animal with no depth.

I'm not a pet cat. I am Sammy Kamau-Williams' double. I gave him my soul. And I locked my breathing onto his. I'm doing the job Lily Williams didn't have the time to finish.

Before I took her place, Lily watched over him every day and every night the Good Lord gave them. She coddled him like a prince until he was twelve. Then, what had to happen happened, and no one could change a thing about it. Up there, the messenger Papa Legba opened a secret door. The Majestic One called her up there to Himself. Lily is no longer of this world, or more precisely, she's turning in orbit around this world.

For the unbelievers, she died in 1961, in the first days of spring. It's written on her death certificate. She's resting for all eternity in a little graveyard eaten away by weeds in the big town of Savannah, in Tennessee, not too far from Nutbush, where the great Tina Turner was born. If I were a sculptor, I would dedicate a bust worthy of Janus to her: on one side the perfect wife and mother; on the other, the fighter, the tormented soul haunted by seven devils.

The only thing she remembered is having seen something extraordinary the morning she died. The rest cannot be told in everyday words. The rest is a private matter.

My Sammy is now over sixty. If I keep watching over him after all these years, it's first of all because he's the flesh of her flesh, the son of Lily Williams' only daughter. And second, because the malevolent forces chose him a long time ago, at the time when he was merely an innocent little creature.

That day, panic-stricken neighbors claimed that our Sammy was grazed by the left hand of the night. They hastened to light candles in the church down the street and bowed to the ground before the holy icons.

For me, this was all nonsense. Why him? After all, Samuel was only an innocent child. I say Samuel because he was named like that in honor of the Jamaican who had been baptized that way when he was in his twelfth year. Wasn't the man the public knows as Sammy, the sixty-two-year-old jazz virtuoso, already in germ in the little Samuel who was the apple of Lily's eye? Unbelievers won't easily see the link between these two persons, on the one hand the child—I would even say, the baby—and on the other the artist who now counts four decades of artistic production, thousands of concerts, a dozen records, and three books. But wait, Sammy is not just a musician. He's also a visionary poet, a precocious writer, and from very early on, a political activist. He also signed two novels and collections of poetry. All written at a tender age, between the age of nineteenth and twenty-three. Hundreds of thousands of you adulate that man, have listened to him for years, and have been blessed by his music. His photos illustrate the jackets of records, magazine covers, and T-shirts. All you have to do is open the first jazz or hip-hop mag to see his life go by like on the gigantic screens in Times Square. But Sammy—our Sammy—is a completely different story.

Let me tell you again because I strongly doubt that you have the long-term, reliable memory of a feline. Her name was Lily. Lily Williams. She had reached the age of a thousand souls. Lily was, is, and will remain the maternal grandmother of the child who will later be known as Sammy Kamau-Williams.

Life had not spared Lily. She was born with nothing in her hands. Not even a straw mattress to sleep on. In her adolescence, shreds of nightmare sealed her eyelids. Her star pointed in one direction only.

Servitude. But if that's what you think, you don't know her.

Lily was a fighter, a fierce activist all her life. Nothing like Nanda, the good maid from the Gulf of Guinea, conquered by the Thing right from the cradle. In any case, she wasn't like those people brought to the African coast blindfolded before being thrown into the hold of the slave ship.

The world is filled with both monsters and pure souls. The Nandas of today are strutting around on the streets of New York. They have traded their ancient fears for timeless indifference. Lonely, even in a crowd, they greet each other with a little nod so they won't have to shake hands and fall into each other's arms.

Naturally, Lily was involved in all the political campaigns for civil rights waged by her people. Like Lily in the past, I, too, have a mission on this earth before I end my life as a wise cat: watching over a man in the grip of the suicidal fever of concerts, struck by the violence of his celebrity. I know everything about him. I see everything. Only unbelievers will dare to contradict me. They make me laugh. Can they acquire the clairvoyance of cats to delve into the mysteries of Nanda's world? What do *they* know about the migration of souls, the intergalactic deserts and the interstellar voyages made at the speed of light?

Nina Little

If, like me, you had the privilege of knowing that great lady, Nina Little, you would have immediately noticed how important dogs were in her life. I won't hide the fact that I'm not crazy about those plodding, stupid creatures. I often wonder what humans can possibly get from them. To me, they're as dirty, noisy and incomprehensible as the demonstrators gathered in Zuccotti Park are to Wall Street traders. But every race has its mysteries and since I'm not a human being and still less a ruthless banker, I keep my reluctance to myself. I must admit, however, that Nina loves her dogs and it must be reciprocal. They are the object of her boundless love. Of her longing for maternity. They are her companions, her beloved children; they light up her existence. And it's highly probable that it has been like that from the first day they met to their last sigh. If my memory is correct, Nina had fox terriers, a boxer, an incredibly clumsy spaniel, and two false twin Chihuahuas.

One day when I didn't have much to do, I got the odd idea of following a dog in the street. For no particular reason. Just to see where it would take me. That dog was a short-legged Australian sheepdog with short ash-gray fur. Trailing him, I took the first street to the right as I came out of my house, then the street to the left, then right again and so on until the dog, who had not noticed my presence, stopped short in front of a gate that led down to the bowels of the earth.

Above this entrance, which didn't look like much, a little sign with the word SUBWAY in white letters on a blue background. The dog rushes into the subway entrance. I follow him, my head swimming. From this day on, I take the subway with a light heart, trying to avoid the advertising posters and the trains that end up in Brooklyn.

Nina's dogs are particularly classy. They're clean, well combed, well dressed and they always have a courteous word in their mouths. At least that's how she described them when we first met.

As for me, I was coming from the sewers. My fur was tousled, my nose snotty, and I was quick to use my claws. Uncontrollable spasms would make me double over. I won't even try to describe the way I ate. Hardly was the dish put in front of me than I'd throw myself at it, dive into the sauce, wade into the gravy, and smear food all over my face. And for my final number, I'd let out three little belches before clearing off. Reaching out like Muhammed Ali, she'd grab me by the throat and make me sit down, gently.

"Hey! Little cat. Cool it!" she whispered the first time, and by the sheer power of her gaze she made me stand still.

I was wild and tried to escape again, but I hadn't considered the elasticity of the lady's forearm. I surrendered. And that day, in a calm but firm voice, Nina gave me my first lesson in manners.

Through patience, I learned how to sit at the table calmly, without rocking my chair, something that really annoyed Nina. I learned to put my napkin away in its ring and into the drawer, do the dishes, and above all, to appreciate the tasty food she can cook better than anyone. Her recipes were transmitted to her orally by her grandmother, who got them from her great-grandmother born in Macon, Georgia.

White rice, red or black beans, pork, pickled herring, corn flour, accra, shrimp fried in palm oil, sweet potatoes, and plantains—I can't get enough of them. Pork was forbidden when I was called Farid and lived in the warm shadow of Islam. That's all changed since my long stay in the sewers of New York. I embraced the change: I accepted it instead of erasing and forgetting it. I buried certain certainties. I used to think chaos was necessary for all forms of creation but now I know it's not true. I am someone else now. I want to be a cat with no other rule in life than the rule of Love. I would add that I am neither from the East nor the West and I do think I'd even eat rhino meat just for its taste if I could find some easily on 125th Street. Don't think I lost my faith—no, it's just that I look at things a bit differently now and I've changed, like everybody else. You never swim twice in the same river, observed an old Greek philosopher. And the swimmer is never the same, say the followers of Buddhism. They understood everything, before all the others. From them, I have retained a little practical lesson: what we see is conditioned by our faculties of perception, which are quite limited. The more we accept that many things escape us and appearances are often deceiving, the less we make hasty judgments. That's what brings calm into our carnal envelope, lowers the collective temperature and strongly encourages peace and tolerance. Since then, I've been feeling lighter.

I have always liked colored pencils and notebooks, book bindings and ink. Nina used to scold me when she caught me with my finger in the inkwell. You're going to dirty up everything, she'd growl. I remained motionless with a blue paw up in the air and a little false tear in the corner of an eye. I would wait till she turned her back to stick my finger, blue with ink, into my mouth. I loved the bitter taste of India ink. I believe I played this little game to an advanced age. Nina was completely fooled. The times she found out what was going on, her features would instantly freeze and her face would turn the color of mercury. She would invariably pull me by the flexible skin of my neck, lift me off the ground, and lecture me. I was afraid of her wrath and yet I would do it again even more as soon as the muscular pain left my neck. The taste of ink was irresistible. As months went by, I learned my lesson, cajoled and tricked her more.

Nina would compliment me, predicting that this time I'd go back to the straight and narrow, back to cleanliness and politeness. I was her little angel once again. Considerate and all. I still wonder today if she put blinders on or if she was pretending just to have some peace.

When you don't have much to expect from life, some people, like Nina, will find the right to be indignant and the strength to ridicule the bitchiness of life deep in their guts. The blues was born from this soil in the plantation fields of the South before reaching the big cities of the North.

It's very early in American history, around 1620, that African slaves land in Virginia. They are among the first immigrants—except that the Africans didn't choose to embark on the slave ships. In the 1700s, there are only thirty thousand Blacks in the British colonies of the New World.

The machine to depopulate the African coasts is running full steam with the complicity of the local chiefs. In 1860, there are 3,800,000 slaves in the southern states. Those figures have risen dramatically through the development of tobacco, rice and cotton farming in Virginia, Mississippi, and Georgia, all the way to the edges of Texas. At the same time, black volunteers enlist in the Union Army, commanded by General Ulysses S. Grant, to go fight the slave-owning South. Nothing will be as it was before. The Civil War changed all that. It leaves behind it 650,000 dead and definitively ruins the economy of the South.

On December 18, 1865, the Thirteenth Amendment to the Constitution puts an end to slavery. A posthumous victory for Abraham Lincoln, assassinated in April of the same year.

James Meredith enters history in 1962 as the first black student admitted to the University of Mississippi. Hawaii, where the young Barack Obama was born one year earlier and where he grew up, shows a more tolerant, more cosmopolitan profile than the old slave-owning South.

Soldiers camp in front of James Meredith's apartment to ensure his security. Every time he goes somewhere, a federal agent accompanies him. In New York and the big cities of the East and the North, the Black Arts Movement (BAM) begins its constant combat. Objective: nothing less than equality and justice. Nothing less than the emancipation of the black people by any means possible, as if to echo the slogan of Malcolm X. Artists, writers, and musicians like Amiri Baraka, Sonia Sanchez, Maya Angelou, and Ishmael Reed will raise BAM to the highest peaks. This is the soil in which Sammy Kamau-Williams plants his first seeds.

In 1974, he composes "Winter in America," a hit played over and over in the ghettos. It makes you feel the long icy coat that covers America, the disorientation and death of all the healers imported from Africa.

Gerald Ford succeeds Richard Nixon, weakened by scandals and the warning shots fired by the young people of America.

My last life had not yet begun. I didn't know the Enchanter existed. And no one had yet tried to end my days by drowning me in a bucket of water sprinkled with bleach.

For a concert given on the campus of Lincoln University by The Last Poets, Sammy and his friend Harry Gibbs concoct a poetic and political medley. It's an immediate hit, first on campus. The Midnight Band was born. Black music has now two new magi in its ranks. That's when the media found a nickname for Sammy. They called him the "Black Bob Dylan." There are worse compliments you could get from these white journalists who quickly run out of ideas.

My old mentor used to say that the nails that crucified Jesus Christ were called Ignorance, Selfishness, Hypocrisy, and Rumor. The journalists did a good job. They smeared Sammy's reputation. Shame, anger, and resentment got the better of his unparalleled bravery. Drugs took over. They waited until alcohol had attacked his skeleton before taking hold of his soul. In the smoking red clay of the Deep South, Papa Legba was waiting for him at the very first crossroad.

In his youth, Sammy was a robust boy, with long legs, a narrow waist, broad shoulders, and a light complexion. He sported an Afro and wore African shirts. Deep inside, he's a child perched high on his legs, surprised by his new morphology (yes, the root of our billions of cells) that will henceforth accompany him like his shadow.

Providence endowed him with the biggest Adam's apple on earth. As soon as he opens his mouth to talk or sing, that's all you can see. The size of a child's fist, it goes up and down his larynx with the regularity of a metronome. His Adam's apple is accentuated by his large tuft of hair and his dark glasses: a jewel in a fine mahogany case. Girls have eyes only for him and men are jealous of the baritone voice surging up from his chest. That voice will not cease to wake the black people, to shake the world with revolutionary refrains and compassionate melodies.

Sammy was born with that gift. He's a shaman who can turn chaos into order. A craftsman of the blues. A *bluesologist*, that's what I am, that's what every fiber of my being makes me, he repeats forcefully to the stupid reporters who describe him as the godfather of hip-hop. That predisposition was evident in him very early on, as soon as he was born. It is given to few people to keep that flame going, to believe in it truly and never to doubt it. And a very small minority knows how to use it, effortlessly—at least in appearance. The rest of life is only a long, patient apprenticeship to succeed in mastering that talent, to use that inner fire without risking one's life. That gift of the gods has its good part and its bad part. Its magic is to be neither good nor bad but to be both at the same time. All the time. From the conflict with evil can come the aspiration to felicity. If evil disappears, even momentarily, the good vanishes. Every blues singer knows this and if he lights a candle it's to cast a shadow, to create a little bit of night that will heal his stigmata. Night is his present and at the end of it, he will find a gleam of hope and the incandescence of the day.

The day is the right hand of the universe, the night, its left hand. Day and night can switch parts, create intermediate zones rich in fog. Getting lost in fog can last a long time. A whole lifetime.

In every way, Sammy is a son of the blues. Wandering poets, the blues singers from the Mississippi Delta carried with them from place to place the memory of the suffering of the slaves, mixing in with it biblical characters and the spirits of the African forests.

Their heartbreaking songs restore the vitality of characters larger than life. The Master of the Crossroads remains a recurring character in this repertory. He was born on the Slave Coast, in Africa. His other name is Papa Legba, from Haiti to Trinidad, from Cuba to Louisiana. In Brazil, he's called Eshu but don't be fooled: it's the same spirit, half man, half god.

He's represented as an emaciated old man smoking a pipe. He's poorly dressed, with an old jute bag slung across his shoulder. He has a limp and walks leaning on a crutch. Children call him Broken-leg-Legba. Watch out, this goblin opens or closes the gate to the other world. He rules over roads and crossroads. He keeps under his beard the secrets of origins, the idioms, customs and animist mores of the deported Africans. He officiates at the crossing of roads and the smoke of his pipe gets the dying back on their feet again. You stiffen up at his view and then start to sing prayers to coax him. Sometimes he lets you through.

Papa Legba
Papa Legba l' uvri bayè pu mwê
Papa Legba pu mwê pasé
Papa Legba

Papa Legba
Papa Legba, open the door,
Papa Legba, let me go through
Papa Legba

A Night of Ecstasy and Downfall
Berlin, Early May 2011

The most beautiful thing we could ever experience is the mystery of things.

Albert Einstein

Everywhere Lily Williams' legs preceded me I feel good. They invited me to trot safely behind her. I must say that I felt particularly great in Berlin, in the company of Sammy and his newly reorganized band. The drummer had left, hired by Odin, a Scandinavian band influenced by gospel piano and Cuban salsa.

Berlin is not the cold, depopulated city drowned in fog that you see in '50s spy movies. For someone who knows how to listen, Berlin is teeming with life day and night. Especially at night. A strange fact for a metropolis crisscrossed by busses, trains, subway lines and yellow cabs, is that the Berlin woods are full of wild animals. Wild boars, deer, reptiles and even wolves are recapturing their lost territory which had been conquered by the human race. I must admit I love the idea that man is no longer the only creature at the center of the city. And a part of the urban space has been taken away from him by his brothers with feathers, wings, palmed feet, and horns makes me even happier. Men, plants, and animals share the city of Berlin from the inside. Berlin, which has nothing of a Western city, of a Babylon with no faith or drive.

I remember its wide streets, its uneven pavement. Its sky sprinkled with stars, peopled with immaterial creatures, permanently inhabited by the human species and by genies. And my inner ear opens in an unusual way. I hear colonies of birds rising to the heavens. I listen to their whistles, their drumbeats, the flapping of their wings. I feel the four teeth of the boar against my flanks. I dread the return of the vulture with a demonic face. In my heart of hearts, I know the Berlin night has nothing frightening for pure creatures who have nothing to fear from life. Keep your personal demons at bay, look at the rest of the world benevolently, and you're okay.

Yes, I remember Berlin. It was just after the bright Paris interlude. Berlin under a rain of stars. If I tried to express myself in a poetic way, I'd say the left hand of the Lord wanted to pour its inkwell over the azure of the Berlin sky. But the right hand did what had to be done. The sky, instead of growing dark, became lovely. Utterly blue. Brilliantly blue.

Under this crystal sky, the Maria am Ostbahnhof club lives up to its reputation: a warm, reinvigorating jazz spot that keeps time in every season. A temple of music.

On the first evening, the audience was very enthusiastic despite the modest attendance. That truly heartened Sammy, who was smiling in a way I've rarely seen him smile since. And it was contagious: it heartened me, too. Like in former times. From the time when I still loved nights in his company. I had the strength to face the fatigue of a tour, the energy needed to carry out my mission on this earth: to remain the cat of that prodigy, Sammy Kamau-Williams.

We saw something extraordinary in Berlin. While the TV cameras of the whole world are turned on Knut, the little polar bear of the Zoologischer Garten, other, more aggressive animals move around silently at nightfall. They don't let themselves be filmed by cameras, camcorders, or cell phones.

The mascot of the Berlin Zoo became a planetary figure in a few days. An emperor. "Kaiser Knut" was the headline in *Bild*, the most lyrical and popular of the German dailies.

I'm jealous of that cub. Sammy made me feel like I was jealous right away. Of course I denied it but not for long. The phenomenon that the world press called Knutmania puts to the test his closest competitors. Those stupid journalists kept repeating that his notoriety outshines the renown of the Queen of England, the fortune of the Pope of Rome or the brilliance of Michael Jackson.

For unbelievers, Knut the polar bear cub was born December 5, 2006. Up there, the Lord, in his infinite bounty, called him to His side on March 19, 2011. I don't know if Papa Legba will allow him, too, to climb to the seventh heaven of the blessed. I imagine the cub will huddle in the arms of Michael Jackson, who died June 25, 2009.

The villa that houses the American Academy of Berlin is in the suburb of Wannsee. Accessible by metro, it's a perfect retreat. So here we are: we've left for Wannsee, its lake, its resort, its calm, deep woods.

We relax, settle down. Lots of space in the villa. Sammy and his whole band sleep or rehearse on the second floor. I chase squirrels in the big park. Something unusual struck me as I played with the squirrels. I would catch them one after the other without much effort. Squirrels are little pests who run all over and take refuge in the treetops in a few seconds. But the squirrels there are strangely slow. I soon realize that they are carrying on their frail shoulders the burden of all past suffering. I soon feel a great compassion for these frightened, powerless squirrels and I realize that the villa has a long history behind it, the kind you can learn in history books.

It belonged to the family of the banker Hans Arnhold, whose tumultuous inheritance coincides with the tragic trajectory of Berlin in the twentieth century. Few cats know that it was in Wannsee, in one of those luxurious hotels around the lake, that the high dignitaries of the Third Reich made the decision to launch the Final Solution and its ensuing calamities. Because of that, the squirrels lost their agility, and perhaps their sleep as well.

From the upstairs windows, I hear a melancholy tune, right out of the trumpet of Chet Baker. I'm shivering.

It's getting late. I leave the squirrels to their suffering. I'm about to go up to my room when, on the stoop, I hear bursts of melancholy notes. The trumpeter has launched into Chet's repertoire.

The American Academy of Berlin invites American researchers and artists who would like to live and work in the capital. The studio I occupy with Sammy is on the second floor. It looks exactly like a little apartment in a Manhattan condo. The whole place is comfortable, spacious, and well furnished. A large bed, a bright living room, a bathroom, and just at the entrance a little kitchenette that suits me perfectly. A Mac connected to the internet, a stereo, and a TV help to attenuate the Spartan look of this residence for monks. The highlight here is the view over the vast well-kept garden, and the lake beyond with yachts gliding lazily over the blue canvas made iridescent by the breeze from the surrounding woods. Classical statues hide beneath the tall oak trees that lead to the steps in front of the villa. The decor keeps reminding you that you're not just anywhere. And that you're probably not just anybody. I really enjoy these tiny instants where I leap up those few steps. For the musicians, though, Wannsee is at the end of the world. As it's a good hour and a half from the city, you need a taxi and a few bills in the back pocket of your pants.

In Berlin, too, Sammy gave us the slip. The villa was too quiet for him. I'm going to see real people closer up, he confided to us in the afternoon but didn't elaborate. Of course, we were extremely worried, but he's so stubborn, you really shouldn't try to stop him. He disappeared toward the end of the afternoon with one of the musicians.

They'd gone to the Savoy Hotel, a fancy establishment in the Charlottenburg neighborhood, not far from the zoo.

The next morning, preceded by a sense of foreboding, we arrive at the hotel early. We thought we'd find Sammy and his musician in the lobby of the Savoy. The musician is all alone. No Sammy. He didn't come down for breakfast, we're told. He isn't in his room either. He must have vanished in the middle of the night, or perhaps at dawn.

No one knows where Sammy's hiding out. The reporters and organizers are worried sick. Where is he? Where the devil did he go? The question ricochets off our foreheads with no answer. Is he hiding in a bar in Prenzlauer Berg, in the beseeching arms of a new lover, or in some cellar, looking for a vein to shoot up?

In the papers, all they talk about is our bear cub. Knut was rejected at birth by his mother Tosca, who herself was born in a zoo in Canada. Scientists admit they don't know why Knut and his nameless brother were abandoned by their mother. Lars, their father, is seven years younger than Tosca. But that doesn't provide sufficient reason to see Tosca deprive her offspring of affection.

We know Lars was born December 12, 1993, in the Munich zoo. Knut and his nameless brother were taken in by zookeepers of the Berlin zoo.

Panic-struck, the two cubs slip all the way back into an inaccessible grotto. It takes two skillful employees with a long fishing rod to remove them from the claws of death. Four days later, the Absolute, in His infinite bounty, called Knut's nameless brother up there to His side. At that moment, I knew that Knut would enjoy an unusual bear's life in Berlin, the city that opens wide its streets and parks to everybody.

Unbelievers strongly believe what they read in their morning papers before having their latte and rushing down into the circular underground metro.

The official press release confirms that a pulmonary infection took away Knut's nameless brother. I won't raise the tip of my nose to persuade them of the contrary. Although much coddled by the personnel of the Zoologischer Garten, Knut is the size of a guinea pig. His life hangs by a thread. It doesn't matter. Great ills demand strong remedies. For forty days, he lives in an incubator. Thomas Dörflein, his guardian angel, watches over him morning, noon and night. He sleeps with him, he eats with him. And above all he plays with him night and day.

Washed, brushed, pampered like a little prince, Knut is presented to the public March 23, 2007. For the unbelievers, that's the day Knut was born. More than three hundred reporters from all over the world take up position in front of the gates of the main Berlin zoo. Flashbulbs crackle for two whole hours. Correspondents with orange armbands write down everything in their little notebooks to comment on this fairytale life. Others are typing away frantically on their laptops while still others are filming Knut's slightest gesture. A paw raised above his head and there's a rush to the edge of the zoo.

March 23, 2007 was baptized Emperor Knut Day, or more prosaically Knut Day. The next evening, thousands of children from Boston to Bangkok fall asleep with a teddy-bear cub the same size and the same snow color as Knut. It's safe to bet these children will grow old and before death grabs them they will ask to be buried with their little teddy bear Knut.

On that day, March 23, 2007, Sammy didn't follow Knut's wild day like everybody else. He didn't learn how Knut was first fed with a bottle by Thomas Dörflein and his colleagues. How he was nursed back to health with food specially prepared for him. Reinvigorating food made with cat food (yum! yum!) and cod liver, spiced up with lots of vitamins. Sammy heard nothing of Knut's two daily visits to the international press, walking like a princess to her coronation with his guardian angel Thomas Dörflein at his heels. A slight hitch in that princely schedule and all the media, panic-stricken, pass the word around and spread dreadful rumors about the cub. Sammy could never have imagined how the media prematurely buried Knut, sealing his fate on April 18, 2016, on the basis of a preposterous story.

That morning, Knut keeps a little out of the way in the enclosure where the public usually watches him strut around. Immediately, a rumor about Knut's fatal illness goes global. The blogosphere gets all agitated. A Japanese TV blabber thinks he knows the polar bear cub won't make it through the night and Japan is in tears. Unbelievers rush to Saint Rita, the patron saint of desperate causes and patients with terminal illnesses. The truth is much simpler. Knut is teething. His upper right canine is sending signals to the cortex. A few hours later, the pain has been forgotten, thanks to the treatment given by the gentle Thomas Dörflein. From Tel Aviv to Rio, children can go back to sleep in the arms of their teddy-bear cub.

Sammy had no idea of all that. He had been unavailable for three whole days and as many nights. The concert at the Maria am Ostbahnhof club is no more than distant memory. He was found unconscious in a cellar in Schönberg. How he found this revolting hole, no one knows. They found a pipe, an ash tray in the form of a plastic Buddha, a sheet of aluminium foil and his lighter right next to him.

He'd fallen off the wagon again.

CD2

Seeing Harlem Again
End of May 2011

Sappho's Thighs

You always leave a good concert slightly dazed, like when you come out of a movie theater rather disoriented because you took the emergency exit without realizing it and you're suddenly back in the tumult and the agitation of the city. You have a hard time regaining your footing. The ghosts you just left give you the impression they're tugging at your sleeve. It is precisely in these moments, at the crossroad of two emotional states, that the Thing attacks you by surprise.

I've rarely seen Sammy as happy as when he was in Paris and Berlin before his relapse. Usually he would look lost, like someone who'd been wallowing in his clothes all day in an unmade bed. But there, he was bright as a button. He hadn't played in public in a long time. Even if he'd say the opposite out of pride and invent imaginary concerts for reporters in the state of Missouri, or in the Kansas City casinos or in the Tennessee of his childhood. The Parisians who saw him at the New Morning first and then at the Parc de la Villette hadn't realized they were giving him a shot of oxygen. Naturally, because he had enchanted them with his unearthly voice. That's our man for you: he had the knack.

In America, his career is studded with exploits, fabulous concerts, prophecies that came true and exceptional collaborations with extraordinary artists of the caliber of Stevie Wonder, Michael Jackson, and Bob Marley. That past is a protective wall that surrounds him and insulates him from the world. That legend is quite handy and profitable for producers and record companies. Sammy, or Sam, as his high school buddies call him today, doesn't live on glory alone. He sometimes doesn't have enough to eat, skips a meal. Swallows his pride and lines up in front of the churches that hand out a bowl of soup to the homeless. Reduced to a thousand tricks to survive like all the black folks who wanted to tell off the America of George Washington as well as the America of George Bush.

In Paris, the audience wanted to taste a new vintage. He was bubbly. Radiating grace. We owe that wonder to a young London producer, Dick Simmons. He waited for his time to join the dance. To tell his story, dazzle music lovers, and remake the world as he wishes. For the moment, patience, the young Brit seems to whisper to us.

Sammy was full of energy. I have forgotten nothing of those precious moments. His denture was in place, the muscles of his jaw completely relaxed. He had his eyes closed and seemed to fly over our heads.

It wasn't just Paris and Berlin. San Francisco, too, was an oasis. He was able to recover, or more precisely, recognize sensations he was familiar with. As if he was receiving the freshness and gaiety of San Francisco Bay through all the pores of his skin. He hadn't played at Café Society for ages.

Unbelievers even wonder if he ever set foot on the West Coast again. Did his steps lead him somewhere else, rather than into a dark cave with stinking, disheveled wrecks like him, all black and Latino? They laughed diabolically, displaying their toothless mouths. Possessed by a frenzy incomprehensible to us regular people, they kept moving frantically, putting their ass on the one chair of the main room only to get up a second later. Others would bring the crack pipe to their lips and fall to the floor. Remain frozen there in a stiff position, the position of a corpse. Sammy lived a whole year among that crowd. It was his road to Damascus, his crossing of the Styx.

Once strong, his voice is now hoarse, rasping. It's halting and breaking as if on the verge of a sob. It is all the more touching. The audience, especially the black audience, is deeply moved by this emaciated, disheveled character, old before his time. A puppet hanging from the fingers of a mischievous, grotesque god: *Baron Samedi* or Baron Saturday, who haunts the graveyards of the New World.

They know what Sammy's been through. Liquor and drugs may have coarsened his features and tobacco fogged up his vocal cords, but on his mask of a revenant they can read a sorrow and a past they've known since that night in the hold of the slave ship.

A tall, well-built redhead, Sappho LeDuc has the prominent cheekbones of Slavic peoples. Her firm, decided steps raise a little cloud of dust behind her. Her eyes may seem hard for people who don't know her. They're always gentle in Sammy's presence. On her sweet face, there's a light, lingering veil of sadness that is never lifted, even on clear days.

One day, in the plane taking him back to Dallas, Sammy starts to shake uncontrollably. He's coughing, his nose is bleeding. Sappho is worried, all the more so because she knows her man has been clean for weeks, in fact months. She tells the flight attendant he's just recovering from a bad case of flu. In fact, he's having withdrawal symptoms. The Thing has been lying in wait for him.

The next day, he's in front of her door. He's wearing a baseball cap pulled down over his nearly bald skull, his gaze lost in the distance. From her stoop, you can see who's coming from afar. He's waiting for his dealer. To the north of Manhattan, there's the human tide, the backwash of the crowd, the zigzags of the taxis. There's a piece of sky and the sea is just a few blocks away. Further on, the icy desert, the snow with its white vultures. The packs of wolves ready to join the first horde of humans.

The silence is sometimes so thick in the apartment that at those moments Sappho has the impression she can hear the wind—light, so light—blowing from the garden onto the bay window.

Sammy smiles at her, a tender and worried smile. Suddenly a cat meows and Sappho jumps, frightened. They laugh together. They immediately put their arms around each other. Life is worth living, with this silence all around. A silence interrupted by the breeze in the garden. Sammy makes love to her with controlled passion and skillful tenderness. And Sappho, in every fiber of her carnal fabric, feels the weight of her man coming alive above her. Yes, she loves Sammy as she has never loved another human being. She is happy. He gives her a lot of pleasure. His affectionate words and skillful moves never give her sensuality any respite. With Sammy in her wake, she maintains her boiler at the best possible temperature. She remembers a game she used to play as a teenager in her far-off country. Especially in winter. Her parents would light a great big wood fire in the chimney. When her parents and her brother weren't in the living room, Sappho would lift up her skirt, open her legs and expose herself to the flames to get aroused before going to bed. This innocent game amused her a lot. Love was burning like a pine log in her chest and between her legs. The long, gloomy winters of New Zealand are no more than a distant memory. And her heart burns with love for Sammy.

All that is far away. The nights are now synonyms of insomnia. Recurrent nightmares. Sammy regularly hears the voice of his mother Bobbie and his grandmother Lily. He can hear their steps, their advice, and their arguments. He's away more and more often, he's afraid of setting foot in his own neighborhood. Who in his right mind would want to find the ghosts of his own parents, buried years ago, inside the first subway station?

"People keep telling me I disappeared for all those years, can you imagine someone disappearing like that," he joked with a reporter once, snapping his fingers before adding in the same playful tone:

"I must have a great talent for disappearances, right?"

And hey, he has an announcement to make to this Scottish journalist who's landed from Edinburgh the night before to snap the portrait of the revenant, on the advice of Walt Hastings, a faithful friend, Sammy's caring publisher and the director of Beacon Books. For once he's conciliatory and the discussion goes on. No point telling you how happy the Scot is! But wait, it gets better. A scoop is in the offing. Sammy lets the whole world know that he's putting the last touches on *The Last Holiday*, a book recounting the campaign to make Martin Luther King Day a national holiday. The *Who's Who* of black American music embarked on a long tour across the country to raise public awareness of the dangers of racism and gather signatures to make a legal paid holiday dedicated to the good Dr. King. A bet he won.

The blacksmith of brotherhood was in the front seats. And rightly so: he had the enormous privilege of shaking the hand of Stevie Wonder, the sponsor of the event, and leading him out to bow to the audience after each concert. *Hotter than July*, Stevie Wonder's last album, marks the great stages of the campaign and harmoniously mixes several influences: soul music, rhythm and blues, and funk. A huge hit in 1980 all over the world.

Between Sammy and Stevie, there is more than respect and admiration, there is fusion. They set up a little game, or more precisely, it's Stevie Wonder who made the rules, by sheer chance—unless Papa Legba is in cahoots with the singer-songwriter of such hits as "Happy Birthday" and "Master Blaster." Stevie Wonder instructed his entourage to never slip him the name of a person who comes to meet him. With his senses always on the alert, this man born practically blind wants to manage all by himself. He wants to feel the presence of the Omniscient closer to him than his jugular vein, separate the wheat from the chaff and keep courtiers at bay. When Sammy is introduced into this very limited circle, Stevie Wonder's face lights up right away. A big smile, warmth, immediate complicity and a cascade of jokes. But there's a little detail that nobody picked up. When Stevie talks to Sammy, he doesn't call him by his name or by a nickname. He only calls out "Aries" or "Ay," identifying him by his Zodiac sign: in the language of Martin Luther King and Barack Obama the name for the Ram is *Aries*. The most intuitive pianist of his generation felt all the elements that went into the composition of Sammy Kamau-Williams' personality; he was extremely sensitive to his principle: fire. The Ram of the second decan is governed by the solar star.

At dawn, after a long night of drunkenness and madness, Sammy confides in his diary before sleeping like a log. He rediscovers the taste for paper and pen from his school years. If history is willing not to let go of him, this will be a precious piece of testimony for future generations.

A Six-Dollar Piano

If Tennessee is the paradise of his childhood, the city of Savannah is its nerve center. The kingdom of innocence. The territory of first steps and first games. When New York annoys him, Sammy always turns to Savannah, Tennessee.

South Cumberland Street.

Right near Lily Williams' house, where Sammy lived all through his childhood, there is a small funeral home. Besides delivering coffins, they organize vigils, celebrations, and burials. They often sing gospels, old hymns, and sometimes they dance around an old piano.

The house is inhabited by immaterial beings who come and go as they wish between the sacred wood of Xogbonou, somewhere in the ancient kingdom of Dahomey, and this city in Tennessee. One can feel the flames of early fires. There, Lily Williams sits majestically on a wicker armchair of the kind you see on the porch of well-off families.

The old piano is on its last legs. It's breaking to pieces, you can feel it at each stroke: each note is preceded by its metallic echo. They talk about getting rid of it tomorrow or very soon. On nights when there's a full moon, Lily welcomes the spirits and other ancestors who disappeared long ago, for she still holds secrets and possesses the language of the rites. Every Thursday afternoon, she leads a profane club, the knitters' club. Old ladies with moist eyes behind thick glasses. The knitters' club acquires the piano for which they paid six dollars—a bargain. Lily has an idea in the back of her head. She wants her Sammy to join her and liven up the gathering. Him on the piano, her with the baton. She'll sing the hymns and under the veil of Christian praise, she will summon the spirits of the old country. He'll accompany her on the piano and he'll sing, in his prepubescent falsetto, old tunes to coax Papa Legba into opening the way to heaven to these poor women. Meanwhile Sammy has to learn the fundamentals.

Praise be to Jesus and the Very Blessed Mary, what do you know! Crystal Faith, an old lady in the neighborhood, agrees to make him swallow four pieces at ten cents a lesson. And now, at the advanced age of eight, there's Sammy playing "What a Friend We Have in Jesus," "Rock of Ages," or "The Old Rugged Cross," to the great delight of the seamstresses.

"He's got talent, that kid, ain't he?"

"Sweet Jesus, music's taken over his small body."

They greet him every Thursday afternoon with a smile on their lips and their eyes wide as melancholy saucers.

Two weeks later, completely by chance, Sammy tunes in to a radio station looping old blues from the Deep

South. It broadcasts from Memphis, the biggest city in Tennessee, a hub for southern music both white and black. Because the old ladies distrust the blues, considered as Satanic music, Sammy found a means of defense. He slips the most prominent features of the blues into the religious music he's asked to play.

He does his scales every day but Thursday. In the meantime, he resorts to cunning and sometimes puts himself in danger. He throws himself into the chords of the Devil as soon as Lily leaves the house, and as soon as she shows up again in the room, he goes back to her hymns and blessings.

Four decades later, he hasn't forgotten a thing about his unorthodox apprenticeship.

"When she was out on the landing I would play what I wanted to play but when she came back I had to slip John Lee Hooker into the texture of 'Rock of Ages,' or a chorus about Jesus into the famous 'Dipper Mouth Blues' by King Oliver," he confessed to the journalists who came probing to probe the source of his influences.

Sammy's grandmother Lily Williams was lucky enough to have known her great-great grandmother, who was born in Africa. She was a very beautiful woman. Tall, with her skin the color of night. She came into the world at the court of a great king. The old woman told the children that the Negroes bought by the Whites did not all become slaves. At the time, in this royal court lit by six torches dipped in okoumé resin, her grandfather was in charge of lighting and salt was a precious product. She said that life was pleasant before the arrival of the soul-eaters but little by little, all joy was extinguished. As soon as night fell, the villages were deserted. The soul-eaters would go out on the prowl, preceded by hyenas, jackals and vultures.

The Negroes did not all become slaves, the old woman repeated for our innocent ears. Captives would often disappear during the voyage. Vanish into thin air, definitively escaping from slavery. They had special ways and fetishes that assured them access to the unknown through steep, dangerous paths.

Growing up with my African parents was an incredible piece of luck, she'd whisper, for from an early age, I had the opportunity to listen to many stories. In those days, said the old lady named Adelina, in order to be a good person you had to acquire supernatural powers. It was the duty of the grandparents to see their grandchildren reach adolescence before they could transmit to them the secrets surrounding the preparation of magic potions. Making fetishes and relics was practiced away from the visible world, in the depths of the forest. And the Blacks of the Coast who were the Whites' allies were extremely interested in supernatural powers. Attracted by the smell of blood, they went searching for fetishes, crisscrossing the deepest reaches of the land, killing everything in their path. But the men of the forest were adept at using the cutlass. Nothing could resist them, not even an assault by a herd of water buffalo. If they happened to be captured by the courtiers of the coast, tied up and ready to be delivered to the Whites, all the men of the forest needed was a magic word for their bonds to be sundered immediately. They fled. Once, twice, ten times. But unfortunately for them, the men of the forest could not all get very far because the Whites would kill them with their long rifles. Others would panic and say to themselves: "We must stay calm because the stick in the hands of the White man can kill an elephant." This is how, said my grandmother's grandmother named Adelina in honor of a Spanish nun, they carried off the men of the forest, defeated by the fetishes of the Whites.

The fugitives would walk deep into the forest, hiding in the Mbelet and Mamfumbi mountains in search of new fetishes. The results did not always measure up. My grandmother Adelina's grandmother had heard that the powers of some of the witch doctors would only awake and work on moonless nights. The white men would hear the far-off growls of the panther that protected the Ouidah court and at the exact same time, the dead body of a slave would begin to jerk around at the bottom of the hold. Frightened, the white men said to themselves: "Look at him! His eyes are coming out of their sockets. He has the hair of a panther. What can we do? He's in a trance." Without delay, the white men would then throw him overboard. At the contact of the water, the spirits would free his fleshly envelope and leave. And the slave, or more exactly his mortal coil, would die of drowning out at sea. While his ethereal part, eternally renewed, returned to the forest just like that, at the snap of a finger. That's what I was told by the grandmother of my grandmother named Adelina in honor of a Spanish nun who came to the assistance of the black people of Florida. And that's what I myself told my little Sammy, baptized Sammy in honor of an ancestor whose face was all spotted with red freckles as if he had come out of an inferno. This black red-headed ancestor had known the Spanish nun. His name was Samuel, too.

Lily was not an ordinary woman. She was a born story-teller. And like the teller of the seven truths, she'd roll out her esoteric tales while keeping their codes and enigmas to herself. Once the story was over, she would pick up her bundle again, spring to her feet and return to her big stainless steel basins. To her sheets and the rest of her wash, for she fed her children and grandchildren with her own two hands covered with soapsuds. All you could do was wait for the next occasion. On summer evenings, there was no lack of spontaneous parties. The grounds and backyard of the church were full to bursting. Weddings, baptisms, harvests, the arrival of new people in the neighborhood, any occasion was matter for celebration. Members of the family, neighbors, tenant farmers of the surrounding towns, wandering singers, parishioners and passing pilgrims would all come together for interminable feasts followed by interminable dances.

The old woman's stories were revealing. Without knowing it, her whole lineage was marked by them in one way or another. Lily was one of those people who could draw her family toward the light, the light of day—to dawns, never to sunsets.

As for Sammy, he loved Harlem as much as he detested New York. He hated New York's coldness, howling crowds, its empty-eyed bureaucrats, swarming belly and constant noise. Everything in the city reminded him of walls, walls, walls, the endless sea of all kinds of fences. Only with Sappho could he find some rest. They never really lived together. Both of them protected their own little corner. He kept the practice of his art to himself and she had her personal agenda. Neither of them could accept any stomping on the other's territory. At the beginning, Sappho half-heartedly brought up the idea of cohabitation but when she saw a flash of madness in Sammy's eyes she retreated and apologized profusely. She still remembers how tender and loving Sammy was after that. He elaborated a ritual that he tried to stick to. As soon as she rang the doorbell, the saraband would start. The inextricable embrace of matter. I'd huddle up in a little corner and watch everything. A voyeur with a tenfold increase of pleasure. I shuddered when he took her right hand for the first time as soon as Sappho came through the door, He then slapped her against his big-boned body and kissed her tenderly. Sappho responded with the same slow and tender kiss. With their fingers entwined, he led her as if from a ballroom to the huge wooden table in the living room to give her a second kiss. Which lasted forever. They gleaned the honey of their lips together. Looking into each other's eyes, they exchanged the food of life and love.

Sammy could go from anger to silence and from laughter to tears for no apparent reason. That afternoon, they inaugurated another ritual to spice up their love games: lounging on the immense couch covered with old leather on which they sometimes sleep when they don't have the strength to walk to the bed.

Even today, passion and communion still dictates their every gesture, their every caress. Half stretched out, with their sides joined and their legs mingled, they dream away on that old couch smelling of sweat. They give themselves to each other, then get up, in turn, to light a cigarette or taste the countless liquors that Sappho brings back from her trips. Bottles bought in the duty-free stores of airports or offered by gallery owners well disposed toward her.

Sammy is playful as a kid on a play-rug. He tells a thousand stories and makes up tricks and riddles. He claims the affectionate part of his personality comes to him from early childhood. The inheritance of the Deep South. The memory of the Negro people from the Mississippi Delta to whom he will erect a monument worthy of the name.

Angel Dust

Winter 2008, back from a long tour on the West Coast from San Diego to Vancouver, through Oakland, Portland and Seattle, Sammy felt enveloped in a dark gown of great fatigue. His inner compass was knocked out of kilter by planes, a different hotel every day, luggage to cart around, concerts always in front of new audiences, sometimes interested but often indifferent. He got mad at his musicians and he was unfair to Sappho, too.

"They claim I can't stand anything anymore," he says, trying to justify himself. Adding: "But you—just look around. Look hard. I can't recognize my country anymore. Even Oakland, the home of the Black Panthers, went back into the mercantile mold. How could people change in such a short time? If they're more and more ignorant, indifferent and sheep-like, it's not *my* fault! You can't tell the real from the phony anymore. You're not touched by anything now. Obviously, my political rabble-rousing doesn't move you anymore, brothers! My music scares you, admit it. And my words, my jokes, they don't give you a bounce like before, am I right?"

"From now on, you'll have to keep your sarcasm to yourself, Sammy! That's what I've been telling myself in the bottom of my heart. There are evenings when the passivity of my closest companions distresses me. And now I feel an immense weariness coming over me. All I want is to go back to Harlem, call Sappho, get back to my cavernous apartment, open a bottle of Cointreau, and watch old comedies on my VCR."

The Theater is the epicenter of the musical and political revolution and it's not far from your nest. It's on 125th Street and more than a theater, it's a temple full of history. Back from your harassing California tour, you quickly return to the fold. You won't even look at the Apollo. You don't give a damn about its posters, its artists, and its programs. You rush home. You'll play boxing matches with Muhammad Ali. He's never too far away, his poster is tacked on the door of your study. Ali crushing Foreman. Ali the dominator who became a Muslim. Like him, you're going to say to hell with everything and throw it all away. People get what they deserve. They should stop coming to cry in your loge. Black America is turning away from the revolution. Seduced by the forces of capitalism, it's going astray and wearing itself out in petty personal quarrels; its prophets preach in the desert of the world. But that's not new either.

The nocturnal tide is rising and you can feel its backwash in your guts. You think of your buddies who died so young. The most realistic ones have mellowed. They go to moneygrubbers and release commercial records for scatterbrained teenagers. You don't want to follow that path; you'd hate yourself for selling out for so little. You have your pride—you were blamed enough for it, Lord knows. Now's not the time to darken the sun of your conscience, Sammy!

The nocturnal tide is there, submerging you again. The tyranny of emotions. You might tip over at any moment. You go from excitement to depression with no warning. You have mood swings. You're unpredictable, aggressive. Bitter. Sour, cynical almost. You're like an old dog. Your cynicism doesn't hurt anyone. There's hardly anyone around you now. You're alone. You converse with your shadow. You tear off the wallpaper in the apartment. You were looking for mikes hidden by the FBI, the CIA, the NYPD, or traitors to the black cause.

You've become pathetic.

You're slowly slipping into marginality. Your old demons are returning in force. In the spring of 2009 you're arrested for using drugs. Back to square one. Prison.

At the infirmary of the Rikers Island penitentiary where you're admitted for acute heartburn, a guard recognized you and sounded the alarm. The tabloids learn that Sammy Kamau-Williams was thrown in jail. But again, they lose track of you in the quicksand of everyday life. More than once you landed in the pen. Unshaved, dazed. Exhausted like the bull that bends its knees after his throat has been slit. You were given up for dead more than once. Your obituary goes around the newsrooms.

The news of your hospitalization spreads like wildfire, lit by little blue devils. The telephone rings all the time. Why do they all come running as soon as the vulture shows its claws? Strange how humans are attracted by blood. Nina, who normally pounds the floor with her platform shoes and pets me profusely, doesn't bother to pick up the phone anymore. She has other worries. Other things to do. She takes care of your small production company: Brouhaha Music, set up in her apartment.

During all these years, Nina was your phoenix, your home base, your refuge. And through her advice and reproaches, a safety rail. The phone could be ringing in a vacuum, we knew you weren't the one calling. We kept quiet about your coming and goings. A few blocks away from your apartment, you may be lying on the cold floor of a cell in Rikers Island, the biggest prison in the city and the whole country. Your fingerprints and anthropometric photos, front and profile, make the headlines of the *New York Post*. You'd think they were dealing with a criminal.

In the neighboring cells, the inmates were betting on your return. They said your dreams wouldn't fly away and the man with the baritone voice can't lie. They said they recognized his cry, a mix of laughter, groans, and held-back sobs.

"I'm a hunted animal," you moan, once your pain has eased.

And you add: "Listen to my cry."

It's not an announcement anymore but a prophecy. Wind, growl, murmur, litany. Commotion: that's what makes Sammy's return to prison so unique.

You know how to talk to people like nobody else and find the right words to help them get back on their feet. Mobilize their attention, revive the flame that went out in the depths of the ghettos. The FBI has been keeping you under surveillance ever since your years of fighting for civil rights. They have a file on you. Your paranoia is not fake because the CIA and the intelligence services know better than you how incandescent your work is, although you've almost forgotten all of it. The correctional authorities fear you like the devil. Like the return of what has been long repressed. They must find a way to ward you off. The guards shut you up by clubbing you in the gums. And the other prisoners listen to you cry. They're frozen in silence. A silence halfway between sacred horror and religious adoration.

People don't drown kittens anymore. They don't make the injection themselves. Someone else takes care of that, a vet or his assistant. They pay for the procedure. A clean, anonymous operation. Painless and professional.

As Lily Williams would say, it's better to appeal to the King of the Last Judgment, to the Master of Worlds, than to his saints and that's why I agreed, after much thinking, to speak out publicly and tell you my side of the truth. To bear witness before the Lord and His creatures and so put an end to falsifications and gossip.

To bear witness and save his soul and mine.

To die in peace when my time comes, in the silence and peace of the Almighty. Meanwhile, I don't care to know what people think of me. I never stopped being a child with a frightened ear, a kitten just out of Mama Velvet Paws' womb. When someone calls me "old cat" I see myself again sucking at my mother's breast or prowling around her and five times out of six, I burst out laughing wildly. Me, a wise old cat! Oh, if you only knew, my friend!

Sammy's departure on a stretcher threw me into a terrible state. Assailed by the torments of an invisible torturer, I feel completely disoriented, as if consciousness had deserted my being. I'm no longer hungry or thirsty. My cup of milk is full. The phone rings obstinately into empty space. The TV has remained on, bathing the room in a bluish, icy halo.

With tense shoulders, Nina put an end to my scanty, dreamless sleep. No snoring tonight. Nina, whom I call little mistress although she's Sammy's age, has a hard time coming out of her torpor, too. She has the wan face of bad days. Her lips are pursed as if she wanted to blow on a spoon of very hot soup.

No matter, I go and huddle against her legs. I'm cold, I'm hot. I'm shivering. Nina picks me up and takes me into her delicate, thin arms. I snuggle into the hollow of her chest. She strokes my spine and reaches up along my neck. There, yes, there, scratch me under the throat. Do you feel my tonsils? I purr with pleasure. I tell myself we are two orphans looking for tenderness and comfort. We miss the third one terribly. His demon is stirring at the bottom of the bottle and waits for the innocent hand that will inadvertently deliver him.

No need to be a genius to know that my master and ally is an extraordinary man. I've always known it. I've always known, too, that he lived from hand to mouth and bore the weight of a heavy burden even in his sleep.

"For days at a time, I could remain in a state close to comatose prostration, without eating or drinking," Sammy told me. "I'd lie on my unmade bed without moving, although I'd be shaken by brief tremors like a pet dog who just had a nightmare on the living-room rug. The next day, with no warning, I would regain strength, spring out of bed, pick up the mattress to lean it against the wall, turn my room upside down, then vanish without saying a single word. I scared people just by staring at them. It was the devil leading the dance, not me," he spat out by way of explanation.

Nina, too, remembers this episode. But unlike me, she kept her cool. All that commotion made me feel uncomfortable. She didn't know what to say or do either but she displayed a reassuring face, though a little anxiety would always linger on it. Her eyes would narrow as if to make them more piercing.

I may be just a cat but she didn't hesitate to share her impressions with me. Impressions isn't the right word. It was something more penetrating, coming from farther away. Something like a certainty sustained by visions and dreams, some interiorized murmur. Nina would tell me in a whisper that it was actually Satan who didn't want to be forgotten. He pushed Sammy around to lead him astray so he could get hold of his soul. Between the two of them, an endless, merciless struggle.

For the unbelievers, that struggle seems like what you might see in a bad TV series. A kind of TV epic set in Roman times, complete with centurions, arenas, and chariots. The viewer knows the ending. He will learn how Sammy has returned to the state of a wild animal. How his childhood wounds were reopened. How much they bleed, how lack of respect, shame, and doubt keep them well irrigated.

"Parasitical thoughts go through my head," he mumbles. "Who am I? Who are they, those people who say they really love me? And the many others working behind my back to bring me down? The ones who are using me day and night? Hatching plans."

He's going through another episode of paranoid delusion. Completely removed from everything.

Throughout the decade, all alone, friendless, he will stubbornly fight to save his skin.

How do I know all that? I'm an old cat, with more than one trick up my sleeve. I'm his guardian angel. I follow him around everywhere, like his shadow. Unfortunately, I'm no help to him in adversity, otherwise I would have given anything to keep my Sammy near me at all times. I would have danced for him with his totem in my hand, while flotillas of swallows filled the sky of Manhattan with their cries. I would have rubbed his skeleton with mustard-seed oil and barley syrup to ward off evil spells. I would have done anything to get him out of Satan's claws. I would never have left him out of my sight.

Well before we went to Paris, I felt Sammy was falling into depression. A terrible depression, one he couldn't manage to drown in the acid of his humor. He was sullen, losing his taste for life. What did it matter if he shot up his arms, his legs or his feet, destroyed himself with liquor, smoked crack, lost his teeth and his hair, was just skin and bone and went mad? He could cry his eyes out, spit on his city with "New York is Killing Me." What does that song say? A lucid assessment: lots of doctors examined his case but none of them could understand why New York was slowly killing him. The remedy: go back to Savannah, to the places of his childhood, to the source of his torments.

He could cry and implore the Almighty. Worry himself sick. Scan the horizon for the slightest sign. Feel his way. Papa Legba, the guardian of the living and the dead, wouldn't hear his cries and his loved ones—including his daughter, his beloved Dahlia—vanished from his landscape one after the other.

Sammy, you're tough. A real social animal. Instinctively, you understand everything. You set up a Plan B. The best way to get back on your feet or destroy yourself. You've lived off the benefits of your gift for a long time without worrying about the rest. You persist in wanting to change life. To break the mental walls that surround the country and shut its inhabitants into separate territories. Love, revolution, the struggle of the Black Panthers, the uprising against apartheid in Johannesburg, your ecological battle before the environment was on anybody's radar—it all ends up in songs and poems. Like the streams of Tennessee, your stanzas go into the cosmic sea. The Divine Song. Everything inspires you. And the battle is everywhere, on every street corner. You work for the advancement of black people. An activist with a mind of steel. Possessed by the need to spread the struggle, that's what you are. But on the battlefield, you forgot the main thing, which can be summed up by this question:

"Where does your gift come from?"

You neglected the gods and the ancestors, the long line of priestesses who saved the secrets and the rites brought from Guinea and Dahomey. Only *Spirits* testifies to this inheritance. One album out of sixteen, you must admit that's not much. You know it, you can feel it, but something stops you from levitating—your pride, no doubt. That's not true for everyone. Look at your peers, what do you see? In homage to the ancestors, John Coltrane composed "Africa / Brass" and "Dakar." Sonny Rollins, Art Blakey, and Illinois Jacquet, his rivals, never failed to bow to that saxophonist-turned-mystic. On the sleeve of the album *A Love Supreme*, Coltrane talks about his new state of mind: "In the year of 1957, I experienced, by the grace of God, a spiritual awakening which led me to a richer, fuller, more productive life. At that time, I humbly asked to be given the means and the privilege of making people happy through music."

Sammy, how could you ignore John Coltrane's seminal lesson for so long? How could you remain insensible to the spiritual call from the Muslim or Buddhist world, which saved a number of your colleagues and sometimes close friends? Converted to Islam, there were dozens if not hundreds of them who used that new religion like a safety valve, to spare themselves the horrors of addiction in the last years before death or redemption.

The Pact with the Devil

A starting point and a point of arrival form a straight path. Add asphalt and the path becomes a road which gives birth to a town. When two roads meet, you get a crossroad.

It's at a crossroad that Robert Johnson may have sealed his fate. The man didn't leave many traces behind him. His stay on this earth is not sufficiently documented to prove his existence.

Skeptics are not the easiest people to convince, but the facts are there. Johnson blazed through this world like a meteorite, time enough to stay briefly among us. I heard his story for the first time in New York and I've learned strange things about him ever since. We know he cooked potatoes on a brazier with chance companions, left a multitude of children behind him on the road, signed a pact with the Horned One, and above all, left his captivating music for our ears to enjoy.

Too simple, some would retort. Others express doubt, tap their fingers on the table and after making many faces, declare that no such man ever existed. No, Robert Johnson never existed! He's the poor invention of an alcoholic old man, argue the unbelievers who prefer to know nothing about the mighty troubadour. About the resonance of his voice, the angelic oval of his face or his song that hangs between emptiness and darkness.

Fairy tales have no more existence than genies do, except in saccharine stories and cheap videogames. Of course, they concede half-heartedly, just about anyone can bear that banal name, but the real Robert Johnson, the blues virtuoso, the man who succeeded in combining the eye and the word, the genius who set the stage alight and burned his life away—could that man be the invention of an inspired joker? Inspired, yes, but facetious all the same.

The proof is that his style of play has been imitated so much it would be almost impossible to determine with certainty that the man we call Robert Johnson invented it. Is he really the inventor of a great technical feat or of that slight delay which is the secret of swing? No, no such thing is reported in scholarly encyclopedias.

The unbelievers are talkative. They chatter away but they enjoy him all the same. There's something even better, they whisper with a conspiratorial air. This Robert Johnson, affirm those who saw the copy of his birth certificate in the sheriff's office, was probably born June 8, 1911 in Hazlehurst, an improbable town in Mississippi. Others claim that the town annexed today to the suburbs of Jackson, the capital of the state, was in the past a most unusual town. In those days, life seemed to be worth living there—except for African Americans.

The nucleus of what will turn into a little anthill of three thousand inhabitants is a bit further upstream: out there on the banks of a bayou called Pierre. In Copiah County, black people, who were so harshly treated in the time of segregation, make up most of the population of this town.

In 1991, a team from the BBC goes out in search of Robert Johnson. They comb the Deep South looking for clues. Dates, place of birth, names of parents—anything they can get. The white icons of music, from Keith Richards to Eric Clapton, magnanimously rush out and display their admiration and affection for this genius who disappeared too soon. Vanished precisely on the day he was to perform at Carnegie Hall in the company of the stars of the times—among them a certain Count Basie. Papa Legba has a flair for drama.

The plot thickens when our investigators follow the lead the troubadour himself has provided: his confessing to a pact with the Devil. Confession, or legend?

And is there a connection between his premature death, or more exactly his murder, and that pact? How many children is our prodigy supposed to have left behind? Did he remain without an heir to give his name to? What illness did his first wife die of? And why can't his eternal resting place be identified? What is hidden behind his coffin? From song to song, from recording to recording, the camera rummages through the past and the present, blending the territories together. It thinks it can identify the women for whom Robert Johnson wrote his songs. The researchers turn over every corner north and south of Mississippi, Arkansas, and Texas and no story emerges. The ghost known under the name of Robert Leroy Johnson remains a ghost.

The unbelievers have an answer for everything. They say the pact with the Devil was just a rumor spread by the parents of his first wife. Virginia Travis is her name and she died of a miscarriage. Mother and baby carried off by the Grim Reaper. Robert Johnson was absent. Disgusted, the young wife's family curses the tramp and his diabolical music.

Guilt-ridden, worn down by liquor, sick of life, the author of "Me and the Devil" displays an increasingly erratic psychological profile. He models his behavior on the image his in-laws gave of him. He thinks he's possessed by the Devil, who haunts the crossroads and roads with forks in them.

Robert Johnson was grazed by the left hand of night. He's supposed to have sold his soul to the Devil like Faust did. It's not the first time that's happened, conclude the skeptics, who share their faith in science with the unbelievers. On the topic of his sudden death, they support the well-worn theory of vengeance.

The composer of "Sweet Home Chicago" had the reputation of picking a woman in the audience and to lavish praise on her in order to seduce her right there and then. It is said that after each concert he left with a different woman. So it's easy to assume, say the unbelievers, that some cuckolded husband or an insulted brother bumped him off. The investigators don't think so. Their documentary doesn't give answers to the enigma of Robert Johnson and his multiple avatars (Robert Morton, Robert Spencer, etc.). In fact, it raises other problems still harder to solve. It brings up another lead: witnesses who supposedly saw the performer being poisoned.

As far as I can recall, the crop that was poor at the start gets richer as research continues. We learn a little more about our man. To the guitar and harmonica virtuoso, we attribute not one, but two sons named Claude and Gregory, a grandson named Richard, three regular women, among them Willie Mae Powell, and a host of admirers, acquaintances, and fellow musicians like Johnny Shines. Childhood friends show themselves to the camera and between admiration and aversion they sew up a fabulous coat to hang on Johnson's silhouette. But that's not all. The death certificate looks like it was very carelessly drawn up.

Of all the people interviewed by the BBC, the man who says the least is a certain Miller Carter, the keeper of the cemetery where Robert Johnson is supposed to have been officially buried. He answers the journalists' questions only by nodding his head or rolling saddened eyes. For Miller Carter knows that there is another grave. And even a third. The left hand of the night knows no boundaries.

If the legend says that Robert Johnson, one of the greatest guitarists of the twentieth century, met the

Devil at a crossroad near the small town of Clarksdale, Mississippi, it doesn't tell us that the Devil is none other than the Yoruba divinity who is sometimes given a dog's head and officiates at crossroads. From the Gulf of Benin to Salvador de Bahia, in Cuba or in the Mississippi Delta, this spirit, or *Orisha*, is called alternately Legba, Elegba, Eshu, or Eshu Elegbara. The power and talent Robert Johnson received in exchange for his soul would then be just another name for the quest for truth. Better still, the rejection of the flesh, relegated to the rank of a sin by Christianity, is turned into a celebration by the tellers of truth who spread their message by playing music.

These messengers of the truth are the first singers of what will later be called the blues. The messengers will have to face three walls, each more impassable than the other.

Scorned by the dominant white culture, which is not inclined to understand the secrets of their art, the blues musicians are ignored by the black bourgeoisie and finally cursed by the most powerful institution of their community: the black Church. The Thing, outraged by the deafness of these three groups, takes it out on the bluesmen. It devours their children one after the other. Some, like me, can recognize it from afar. It is preceded by a two-headed vulture.

Coma

I remember an ugly old cat from my years of wandering. His coat stank, his ears hung down and his eyes were evasive. They said he was once proud and smug, dominating and condescending. He was a cat from the rings, an ace in boxing. At the height of his fame he was nicknamed Foreman. But the punches he took through the years got the better of his head.

He was half crazy, constantly escaping his family's vigilance. They'd pinned his address on his hoary torso, an apartment in the wealthy neighborhood of the Upper East Side. He would often get lost in the labyrinth of his past, playing over the movie of the fights he'd lost or won a few decades back. Weakened as he was, he was still respected, for we were still afraid of his uppercut. When he meowed, the polar rustling coming out of his belly filled the alleys of my childhood. I'm sure he survived. He had the resources to weather any storm.

Letting the currents decide their fate was the wisdom that spurred millions of African slaves. Letting yourself be transported by the ocean, the better to access the country of memory, the country of darkness, the residence of the dead for all eternity—that was their route.

Those slaves were innocent, strangers to evil. Their fate was suspended by a thread: the currents of the ocean. To reach Cuba, the Bahamas, Port of Spain or Charleston, what did it matter. Everywhere the same chains, sugar cane and cotton. Everywhere the same rotten luck. Yesterday and today.

Spring 2007. On the day of his fifty-eighth birthday, Sammy got out of the Rikers Island jail. His silhouette: razor-thin. If prison played tricks on him and ate up his time, it didn't affect him deeply. He has a gift for survival: others killed themselves after a spin in the pen. Not Sammy.

The knot of an individual like Sammy is not made with one single string. It's not a corset or a suit of rigid, irremovable armor. It's a supple, fluid shape, always in a state of becoming. A breath, a strong wind you keep seeking. You watch out for it and you welcome it. Like the son who leaves his parents' home but often comes back there in thought; the identity of a virtuoso is made like that, it's something that gets lost but keeps renewing itself in an incessant movement of departure and return. You don't possess your identity like you possess a fetish from yesterday or a piece of property.

In prison, he worked a lot on his texts, composed melodies, memorized other people's tunes, slept a lot, talked as much, kept up his muscles by lifting iron bars and spoke of the passing of time the way you might describe a long drawn-out season.

When he got out, Nina and I were there to welcome him in front of the big gate. I was growling with joy, the high note stuck in my throat, and I went to huddle into Sammy's fleshless arms. Nobody's here for you, Nina whispered in his ear. Except Lily's ghost. That made him laugh.

Lily's ghost. You haven't seen it. Admit it, Sammy! It makes me sad when I think about it. You haven't seen it in a long time. She warned you, ever since you were a very small child. She said to you, watch out for the deadly sins. Be wary of lures, femmes fatales, money too easily earned. Sammy, above all be wary of yourself, of the snake coiled in your belly. You are your own worst enemy. Be wary of your talent, it will surely bring you trouble as big as clouds. Don't forget that most people only believe what they see. Unbelievers and fools only believe what they can hold firmly in their hands. They're not able to retain the real names of things and people. They're not like you, Sammy, who went out to hunt the secrets of the divine.

That's what I wanted to declare to him. But I didn't dare. I kept quiet, keeping my reproaches for myself alone.

He's alive again, able to put one foot in front of the other. Able to tear himself from the flowing clay. Falling and getting up. Falling and getting up again. His lower limbs still stiff from his long stay in the tunnel of numbness, but no matter: blood is beating again in his veins and air is firing up his lungs.

Everything must be relearned at the end of the years of dark night and opaque fog. The simplest gestures, like raising a spoon to his mouth, to the ABC of the language of men. Forget those from before, his brothers in combat, the comrades who died of an overdose, the poets of the street defeated by the winter of the Bush years.

Forget the living dead all skin and bones, the indistinct dust of all those who fell or got burned. Sometimes Sammy can't tell where he put his clairvoyance. He agrees to lay down his arms, to let himself die a second time. He has nothing to explain, nothing to understand. "Don't Explain," his muse Billie Holiday would purr, carried away by heroin.

And it's so discouraging for his loved ones. I'm no longer of this world, he seems to be whispering to us, and yet I stubbornly keep at it. I keep sinking but I would never let go of this crappy life. I would dive into the burning lava of crack, I'd burn up every cell in my body, every particle of the universe for a last puff. A final high. Sammy has left the rails of existence for the shore of survival. He's one with it.

I hope it's the last time he'll feel like breathing his own breath as if it were his last, the last time we'll come get him at the steps of a prison.

He still has to find work. And right away. The owner of the New York club SOB (Sounds of Brazil) was always faithful to Sammy in the past. Between two tours, his steps would take him to the SOB where, despite his absences and his abuse of narcotics, the manager was only too happy to take him back. Sammy was a pole of attraction. The SOB was full every night. Sammy would come home at dawn, exhausted but radiant. He was dragging his long carcass around, feeling out the horizon with the tip of his feet, dancing on the razor's edge. I hope the SOB will open its door to him again.

Once he's passed sixty, man no longer needs to fear the earth. For the earth is reminding him of her, proclaiming she has always been there for him and she's quietly, patiently waiting. At every step, it pulls him to her, saying:

"Don't be afraid, go to sleep, I won't hurt you, just try, my man, go to sleep!"

Sammy is now over sixty; he thought death was at the end of the path a number of times, at the tip of the syringe or in the curls of smoke. But every time death got out of the way and let him through.

Whether you drown cats in a bucket of chlorinated, soapy water or give them a shot at the vet's, the method doesn't matter. In the end, we all croak. A bag of bones that will be thrown into the bottom of a hole, forgotten, and the account settled.

Sammy would have liked to rewrite the history of Savannah and get rid of the bonds of the past. He would have liked to be released from the chains of long ago, freed from his own shadow. Freed from Lily, his grandmother who closed her arms around him as she slipped into death to drag him into the great night with her.

Sammy may recount this trauma in his songs, his books and his interviews all he wants, he can't break the forks of fate all alone and free himself from his straitjacket.

When he was twelve, Lily died in his arms one morning as the sky displayed funereal garlands of black crepe. Sammy instantly began to stammer. He'll say later that since that morning a part of him is bathed in blood and the other is under the spell of dreams. One part haunted by the stiffened carcass of the old woman with drool on her lips, the other part invested by the great voices of the blues.

Lily visits him every night, or almost. Here's Lily draped in a long white tunic, her mop of hair rolled up in a white scarf. She performs a secret dance, turning on herself with her neck anchored on her shoulders, her arms above her head, her left forearm slightly bent. She dances and dances to the point of trance. On the ground, her open feet draw large circles, her dress spiraling around her. And when the dance stops as if by itself, she's on her knees. Breathing deeply. Drawing subterranean forces from the ground. She seems to be sharpening a long blade with a big black stone, round as an Alabama watermelon, picked from the bottom of the ocean. She mumbles strange words to herself, a prayer from way back:

> *A door closes here,*
> *Another opens there.*
> *When the darkness is there,*
> *The horse must let himself be mounted.*

Her lips barely open while her right hand keeps sharpening the blade. She prays and watches and weeps.

> *Sleep, my sweet angel.*
> *Sleep in my arms.*
> *The vulture doesn't know it*
> *But my mount knows where it's going.*
> *Sleep, my sweet angel, sleep.*

Lily Williams unreels her story, her lips moving slightly.

Your task will be to clear and decipher the world by singing its mystery.

You will be a master of the word, a genius of music, my dear grandson.

A raw genius, without wrapping or filter.

I will not be present at your funeral as I was not physically present at your birth.

No matter. Many matronly women with hair white as cotton leaned over your cradle, first in Chicago in the little room where you gave your first cry and then in Tennessee where you bloomed at my side.

And you were the apple of my eye, the joints of my skeleton, the muscles of my legs, and the joy that lights up my neurons.

For twelve springs and as many winters, autumns and summers, you were mine and I was yours, my dear Sammy. We were never two anchors working back to back; quite the contrary, we were one vehicle. Your pain, mine. When you were little, you had such migraines. Sudden, blinding.

You would remain shut up for days and days in the little back room.

Oh! Those constant migraines! They could drive the horses grazing in the meadow behind Mr. Batouque's shack crazy. Mr. Batouque was a peerless craftsman. Silent and distrustful by day, whether in the fields or in his tiny blacksmith's shop. Talkative and warm by night when he'd put on his tunic and became the reverend whose task was to lead the service and liven up all kinds of celebrations. Legend has it that you owe your first music lesson to Mr. Batouque who, by then, was more than ninety-four years old. Some even said he was past a hundred. Whatever his real age might have been, he was hale and hearty and didn't seem to suffer from the thick, muggy summers, so heavy in this part of Tennessee.

Mr. Batouque was a star, he had repelled and defeated many monsters. He didn't speak with other people, he praised life. He ate words, minced them, with solemnity. He was a sublime member of the race of word-eaters.

A musician and an activist for the human race, of course. You can't leave your loved ones by the side of the road and remain silent. You'll carve out the great song of the revolution.

"This Revolution Will Not Be Televised."

Yes, the great revolution of the black people of the Americas, the one more modestly referred to as the Civil Rights Movement, you'll be the one, you with a few other comrades, to sculpt and shape it.

In words. In songs.

You must lead a healthy life, educate your offspring, and keep in touch with your ancestors. Eat healthy food. Five fruits a day. Go to bed early and get up early. That's the price you'll have to pay for the revolution to happen before your eyes, in your lifetime.

You were born a magus, you will die a magus. You are able to retain the true name of things and beings. The great spiritual fever will choose your throat to find its way. To reach thousands of young people who are just waiting for the spark that will send them into the streets.

With your brotherhood, your voice and your instruments, you are the embodiment of that spark. That's what street art is, the art of the poor, ridden with all kind of diseases. That way of weaving your personal destiny into the adventure of all your brothers and sisters—that will remain

your signature. You never stopped readjusting themes and variations, warning of the fires that won't fail to explode as you pass through Harlem, the poor farmers' South and the slum-dwellers' North.

You unmade and remade the labyrinth where the first black slave was lost, you reconstituted the great drum of memory piece by piece. Naked feet, powdered with dust, putting off the fateful time of their return day after day— those feet have no secrets for you. Like the Thing that gnaws at your conscience and haunts your brain. It rose from the depths of time, it's always at your side like a faithful dog, a dog even more faithful than Sappho, the woman of your later years. Sappho, more a nurse than a mistress. Sappho LeDuc, who would gladly have traded her family name of French origin, probably Acadian, for the double Kamau-Williams, half Jamaican, half Afro-American. A double name between two bodies of water. On one side, the strict mother. On the other, the absent father.

Sappho loves you dearly. She offers you her heart. She would like to share your bed. Give you her soul. Of course you'll do nothing of the kind, you don't have the strength to marry anyone, not even Sappho, who breathes out a sweet caramel perfume.

Sooner or later, you'll find the warrior's rest. You did well to spread the Divine Song.

Sammy is in a deep coma. Nobody came to visit him except poor Sappho LeDuc, who Sammy treated so badly. Sappho left of her own free will. As soon as she was gone, I let Nina go back to her place because she didn't have the strength to drag herself through the long corridors of the hospital and she knew she'd be more useful at the office. It took her some time to agree. Not easy to convince her when she has an idea rooted in her head.

"The Day of the Dead, O Lord, pray for us poor mortals!" she sighed as she turned on her heels. I've known her to be more vigorous. In other circumstances, she would have told some of her profound and mysterious stories, known only to her; she would have revealed how our earth is not the whole world and creations necessarily communicate with each other. Then, she would have added: "Let us oppose human unity to the violence of nature. Everywhere unknown forces burst out and propagate evil, let men stand united and do some good." On these words, she would have fallen silent and I would have bowed before her with one paw stretched out in front of me and my muzzle grazing the floor. Nina has a way of being that contrasts with the rest of the world. A way she has of being dignified and noble. Of sustaining the duel of staring eyes.

I walked over to my Sammy. Motionless, his eyes are closed, his face is calm. The hint of a smile on his lips.

My presence and the presence of his grandmother Lily Williams are keeping him alive, I'm sure of it. With his eyelids still sticky from the precipitate of his agitated dreams, he turns to me. He has the eyes of a sad spaniel seeking to be comforted. He's very thin. A sack of bones wrapped up in white woolen pajamas that blends with the white sheets of the bed. Everything is white. Shroud white, coffin white, or the color of a pale, white dawn. I have the feeling he's following my thoughts, although no word has come out of my mouth yet. They've pepped him up a bit. He folds up his legs as if preparing to sit up. But that's asking too much of his body. He gives up. Starts breathing calmly again. His breath is more regular, more reassuring. And then, as if to contrast with the silence of the hospital, the trickle of a voice comes through his lips. To capture the words falling drop by drop from them, I have to lean over him.

The earth is beautiful and good and luminous but that's not all. The earth is also dark and terrible and cruel. And the evil that smothers everything comes from places where men adore wealth and bow before it. Don't worry, my dear Sammy, I tell him, making big signs so he could understand me, I'm here at your side. I'm watching over you. The best of my soul is dust fluttering over your body, I whisper to him. Go back to sleep, my friend. Resist the pain as you always did. Bend your knee only before the Lord, kiss only His lips. Unbelievers think it's a sign of weakness. Don't believe a word of it. The ascetic man you scorned, the beggar you drove away, the wise man you ignored, they are now filled with His love, drunk with His desire. Go back to sleep, my dear Sammy, go back to sleep! You'll regain peace, you'll be reconciled with your inner child. For you, the hardest part is over. The hardest part is behind you.

Your music is waiting for you. Long and straight as the shadow of evening. Your generous music will shower you with sparkling stars. It will carry you back to the native land, before your birth, on the Slave Coast. Then on that cursed land where your ancestors wandered endlessly through the cotton fields. They howled at the moon. Howled and howled and howled again.

In the noiseless, starless nights, in the other world, you will wear a mask of wax that will never scrape the horizon. There are men who continue to exist after death and whose consciousness will never be extinct. Even when the world is haunted, when all is only fear. You come from that family, sacred and singular. You attract young people, you attract birds, chrysalises, and butterflies. You are a theater open to the four winds. Like Robert Johnson, your star shines in the firmament of the blues.

Robert Johnson, the man with hollow cheeks and burning eyes. Who attracts audiences and drives them away. He had a life full of holes, alternating between descents into the night and rebirths. He had to sing or die.

Listen to me, Sammy. You will die, perhaps this very evening. You won't live forever; not you, not anybody. No one is immortal. But we're the only ones to know that we must disappear. Some animals know this by instinct. Knut, the little polar bear, who held the whole planet in suspense for a time, did not have this gift! And it is a precious gift: it's our chance to come to terms with ourselves. In fact, we only possess what we know we must lose, what we accept losing.

All of a sudden, I have the clear sensation that Sammy can hear my words and he's accepting my arguments. Better still, he understands them. He instinctively understands the ancestral wisdom of the motherly black women who care about their offspring's daily bread as they do about the harmony of the universe. They take charge of the quilombos, they manage them with a compassionate hand, a therapeutic hand.

Reginald Kamau, his own father, left the world of soccer and its false pleasures. He retired into a quilombo, a sanctuary near Bahia. He confesses that he found there a place to rest his body and calm his spirit. He wishes his son, too, can regain his mental balance and follow, at last, the path that leads to his inner child, the path of union and ecstasy.

An old Persian proverb attests that the Spirit blows where it will but honor goes where it must. Here, honor has a name: Quilombo.

Quilombo was first the name of a city in Angola before it designated the communities of fugitive black slaves in Brazil and elsewhere. The most famous quilombo turned itself into a republic. The Republic of

Palmares, founded by a maroon slave by the name of Zumbi and wiped out by the cannons of the slave-owning government a few decades later.

The name Zumbi dos Palmares resonates throughout the Americas; its blood flowed for all enslaved people. It is resounding in this room, if only through the intervention of Reginald Kamau.

Listen to the ney, the reed flute grieve,
it tells the story of our separations.
Since I was severed from the bed of reeds,
my cry makes men and women lament.
I need the heart that is torn by parting
to pour into it the pain of heartache and desire.
Whoever finds himself far from home
looks forward to the day of reunion.
As for me, I wailed in every gathering;
I joined with those who were sad and happy, both.
Each understood me with his own feelings,
but none sought to find my inner secret.
My secret is not so far from my lament,
but eye and ear do not know how to see it.

Mawlana Rumi

Sammy left us this morning as dawn was turning amber and gray. He burned up the very last drop of oil in his vital lamp. Anger took hold of me, but thank God, let go of me immediately. I was in the tight grip of anguish and cried all the tears of the earth. My vibrissae still bristle just thinking about it. That Friday, May 27, 2011 will remain carved in the marble of my memory.

Everything has an end. I'm going to close my journal but, unbeknownst to you, the fire I lit in the deepest of darkness will continue its work. The pages of this journal have intruded inside you, through diffusion or contamination. I strove to keep the narrative line as straight as possible and keep judgments and personal commentary on the Enchanter's conduct to myself. My opinion is of no great importance since my goal was simply to present the man as I knew him and not scrutinize his acts or strain them through some moral filter. Luckily, I took my precautions. I noted every detail as faithfully as possible so that history may retain a palpable trace of the life of Sammy Kamau-Williams.

Finally, I express the hope that his most fervent admirers will forgive me for having so succinctly represented a personality as complex as it is remarkable. If this spray of memories had only one merit, it would be the sincerity of their tone.

Animals have entered the human imagination for a long time by playing the role of messengers, and what's more, by being bearers of promises. Since the dawn of time, animals have incarnated the only exteriority and objectivity humans can perceive. That's why the human race has long considered animals as intimate friends, like Knut, or as relatives, and not as substitute objects or fetishes à la Walt Disney.

Dear reader, I miss you already. Not having you at my side anymore is a kind of premature death. Let me kiss you on both cheeks, tenderly.

I am waiting, in my turn, for the vulture to arrive. For him to put his wings on the roof. I am ready and he knows it. I will receive him serenely.

You humans have an odd way of seeing and reading the world—through your brain and your mouth as much as through your eyes. And yet you only see the bark of the world, not its nucleus. You forget that nothing stops, the wheel keeps turning. I don't live in a country, I don't even live on earth. The heart of those we love is our real home.

I hope I've succeeded in covering the nudity of Sammy Kamau-Williams by sewing for him a suit made to his measure. As for the rest, all right, I'll stay here and wait quietly for the wing of the vulture, telling my beads. Yes, waiting, that's all. For the real adventure is invisible and internal. And true greatness is more in being than in expertise. I will strive relentlessly to seek spiritual things, the only things that last—the dazzling flash that surges from The Living. I will make mine the advice of Mawlana, which is also hidden in the Holy Koran:

"Look through the darkness of material life and the brilliant star will guide you toward the garden of real, eternal beauty."

Let me tell you a last, edifying story. One day in the tenth century, sitting in the shade of a vigorous pomegranate tree, a disciple of the Muslim mystic Abou Bakr al-Chibli was relating this:

"God made me come before Him and told me:

" 'Do you know why I granted you my forgiveness?'

" 'It's because I prayed a great deal.'

" 'No.'

" 'Because I fasted a lot?'

" 'Not that, either. It's because on a winter evening you picked up an abandoned cat, and warmed her up in your coat.'"

You can guess the rest. Eleven centuries later, Sammy Kamau-Williams, a bankrupt idealist, who'd seen it all and was rejected by everyone, picked me up in the street and gave me food and shelter. Without asking anything in return, he warmed me up in his coat. Every man, good or bad, is the depository of a fragment of the Divine Song. Despite his faults and his difficult personality, Sammy Kamau-Williams was basically a good person. As the time has come for us to part, it may not be too presumptuous to think that the Generous One just granted him His forgiveness.

People assume that a cat, whatever his age and pedigree, must hunt mice. All my life, with everyone's help, I gave the lie to this axiom. Every being exists not only in itself, but also in relation to others and especially in relation to its Creator. Instead of hunting rats, I made the gift of my small person by putting myself at others' service, mainly Sammy's. I took care of others before taking care of myself and I found inner peace again at the threshold of my last life. When my time comes I will leave this earth—the world of appearances—with a light heart and a smile on my lips.

But I've talked enough about myself!

On March 19, 2011, Dick Simmons, the young British record producer, gets a phone call while strolling about the aisles of Foyles Bookstore, which is spread along the great thoroughfare of Charing Cross in London. There, he finds old, rare vinyl records for his alchemical work.

He celebrated his thirtieth birthday the night before and his cellphone rings every ten minutes. The producer of XL Records keeps tapping frantically on the keyboard of his smartphone to call back the correspondent, identified immediately. A stroke of luck: the gravelly voice of Sammy Kamau-Williams surrounds him warmly. He talks for over an hour with the man he considers not only a musical genius, but also his spiritual father. He's in seventh heaven. He'll say later that this conversation about everything and anything with the author of *Spirits* was the icing on his birthday cake. Ever since he was a teenager, Dick Simmons has harbored a deep admiration for the alchemist. He has lavished demonstrative signs of friendship and respect on him from afar. Visiting him in jail several times and giving him patience and confidence again revived his career and Simmons is quite proud about that. The result is known to all: *I'm New Here*. More than a twenty-nine-minute album. A masterpiece that puts Sammy's voice and words back in orbit, the fraternal essence of the charismatic poet who didn't expect anything from the terrestrial world anymore. As for me, faithful to my avatars, I must bear witness to the facts. When my master and ally stopped conversing with the young producer, he miraculously managed to get up. His eyes regained their brightness, as his visual cortex was apparently intact. Blood reappeared in his cheeks and lips, and sap and vigor flowed back to his limbs. He smiled at me as if to reassure me. He did not open his mouth but I could hear, one by one, the words whirling over his head, unable to make their way to his mouth or vocal cords.

"I would have remained inert, paralyzed, and a dying man if God hadn't sent Dick to rescue me: you are my witness! You'll let the world know that I'm leaving in peace. From now on that will be your mission."

No word came out of his mouth after that. Silence dragged on in the room of St. James Hospital, crushing and imposing, and none of us were able to break it.

The funeral of my friend and master took place in a chapel of the famous Riverside Baptist Church between 120th and 122nd Streets. A dense crowd was standing on the esplanade an hour before the service. There were over three hundred people inside and as many out. Curious onlookers, friends, neighbors or well-known artists, they were all there to accompany him on his last voyage.

I had slipped under Nina's feet, in the first row. I'd made myself small and kept quiet under Miss Little's seat. Her two legs in black tights framed my field of vision. The atmosphere was festive, a cathartic magic. Tears flowed unrestrained but without sadness. Faces remained radiant; the altar, majestic. It was also a parade of stars even though this house of God had had its share of historic events; its sparkling organ had accompanied the speeches of some of the great leaders of this world like Martin Luther King Jr., Nelson Mandela, Fidel Castro, and Kofi Annan.

That first Thursday of the month of June 2011 was a day like no other. Harlem was celebrating its son who had passed away six days earlier. Salvos of memories, showers of testimonials, Sammy's songs and poems, few horns honking. The mike went from hand to hand. On the stage, the musicians got into place. They began to play in an indescribable hubbub. And suddenly, a luminous, clear silence, offered to each and all. Layers of harmony arose, spread out, stretched, wound around in space, gliding over the audience. It was contagious. They all became animated, a wave of joy that would keep on shining even in the darkest of nights.

Extremely moved but very dignified, Sheila Jameela, Dahlia's mother, got up on stage. No affectation, no posture, just a presence. She told us how she met her man: through a common friend, the basketball player Kareem Abdul-Jabbar. Then she passed the baton to her Dahlia, who gave the most moving testimonial to her father. As a poet, in her own words and with absolute gentleness, she expressed all her affection, before passing the mike to a Kanye West strapped into a coal-black suit. Above the forest of microphones held out by the horde of reporters, the young artist recalled how much the music of my master and ally had nourished him. If I'm at the top of my art today, it's thanks to the genius of Sammy Kamau-Williams, he admitted, with a sob in his voice. Then he gave an a cappella version of "We Almost Lost Detroit," full of absolute respect and love. It made my fur bristle, from my muzzle to my paws. Nothing but tears of joy. I followed the crowd in silence.

In front of the church, I recognized familiar profiles, others less well known who I had nonetheless seen on record jackets or press clippings. The good doctor Ronald Jones was there, with admirable dignity.

Abiodun Oyewole, his long-time buddy and one of the lungs of the '70s' group The Last Poets, had taken a night train to be there early. Some, like Walt Hastings, the Scottish publisher and forever accomplice, had come from further away, from Glasgow, the Caribbean or elsewhere. Others still, who couldn't come, did not fail to send a bouquet of flowers or a message of condolence. In a few hours, a tide propagated by social media spread out over Manhattan. From Harlem, the wave reached Paris and Tokyo in no time. Everywhere, the same palpable emotion, the same compassion.

The stars of the rap and hip-hop scene gave all they had to celebrate the memory of their godfather with calmness and determination. Obstacles and unexpected problems have never put the patience of his epigones to test. Radios took the records of the black prophet out of purgatory. Concerts were prepared in Europe, in the United States, in Brazil and Jamaica. As for Sammy Kamau-Williams, he's resting six feet under earth and silence in the Kensico cemetery of Westchester County, thirty-odd miles from his beloved Harlem and far from the red earth of Tennessee.

Today, a year after his death, his three books have been re-edited. His memoirs published with the title *The Last Holiday* were immediately translated into several languages. Homages pour in from the four corners of the world. Prizes have been posthumously awarded and symbolically given to the artist's children. Reunited, for once, the family set up a foundation in his name. Soon streets and schools will perpetuate the memory of the old man with long, skinny limbs, a dirty cap stuck between two tufts of scattered white hair on either side of his tanned skull. Millions of people became fond of the angry young man who composed, one day in 1970, a song of divine wrath: "The Revolution Will Not Be Televised."

As for me, his humble servant, I did everything I could to save a fragment of his soul and mine. I don't know if I accomplished my mission or if I failed miserably.

No matter, the main thing is elsewhere.

Sammy Kamau-Williams is not dead, he has met his Lord. He orbits the Earth in huge circles. Consumed by love, I follow him from afar in thought. I am at his side, silent and serene, concentrating only on my breath—inhaling and exhaling—and as if by magic, all the rest is erased: attachments, sensations, the outside world. I am absorbed by a silence and a peace that nothing can disturb. I am the same and I am another, I am of every sex, I am here and elsewhere, as much in darkness as in light. And that's perfectly fine.

STATEMENT OF INTENT, SOURCES

The substance of this novel comes partly from the life and artistic career of the African American singer, composer, poet, and novelist Gil Scott-Heron (1949–2011). His written work includes four novels and an autobiographical narrative: *The Last Holiday*, published posthumously in 2012. His lyrics, texts, and music accompanied us as we wrote this novel. However, there was no question of writing the biography of Gil Scott-Heron: he took care of that himself. Besides, our imagination is rebellious enough not to be content with confining itself within the borders of this great artist's life. We followed the steep paths of fiction— jubilantly—and as we did so, we touched upon a few past and present spiritual traditions. Any obvious omission or blunder can be attributed to us, for we are not in quest of perfection.

The story of the elephant is told in the *Mesnevi* of Rumi; Merkez Efendi's story is told by Annemarie Schimmel (*Mystical Dimensions of Islam*, University of North Carolina Press, 1975.)

The story of the miser is borrowed from Farid-ud-Din 'Attar (*The Conference of the Birds: A Sufi Allegory*, 1177), translated from the Persian by Sholeh Wolpè (Norton, 2017) and the last anecdote from Amadou Hampâté Bâ (*Vie et enseignement de Tierno Bokar*, 1980); in English: *A Spirit of Tolerance*: *the Inspiring Life of Tierno Bokar*, translated from the French by Jane Fatima Casewit (World Wisdom, 2008). Lastly, the poem by Abdellatif Laâbi comes from his collection *Zone de turbulences* (La Différence, 2012).